THE LEGACY SERIES

SERIES TITLES

The Divide
Evan Morgan Williams

Release of Information
Kali White VanBaale

Neon Steel
Jennifer Maritza McCauley

How We Do Things Here
Matt Cashion

Yes, No, I Don't Know
Kathryn Gahl

The Price of Their Toys
John Loonam

The Caged Man
Calvin Mills

A Day Doesn't Go By When I Don't Have Regrets
J. Malcolm Garcia

These Are My People
Steve Fox

We Should Be Somewhere by Now
Stephen Tuttle

Burner and Other Stories
Katrina Denza

The Plan of Chicago
Barry Pearce

Trust Issues
K.P. Davis

Adult Children
Laurence Klavan

Guardians & Saints
Diane Josefowicz

Western Terminus: Stories and A Novella
Michael Keefe

Hoist House: A Novella & Stories
Jenny Robertson

Finding the Bones: Stories & A Novella
Nikki Kallio

Self-Defense
Corey Mertes

Where Are Your People From?
James B. De Monte

Sometimes Creek
Steve Fox

The Plagues
Joe Baumann

The Clayfields
Elise Gregory

Kind of Blue
Christopher Chambers

Evangelina Everyday
Dawn Burns

Township
Jamie Lyn Smith

Responsible Adults
Patricia Ann McNair

Great Escapes from Detroit
Joseph O'Malley

Nothing to Lose
Kim Suhr

The Appointed Hour
Susanne Davis

In one taut moment after another, Williams lays bare the lives of everyday people stuck on the wrong side of literal and metaphorical divides, often of their own making, that they're unable to overcome their own worst instincts to bridge. Sparse and honest, these stories reveal the flawed humanity of his characters and of ourselves. Insightful, compelling, and beautifully written, this is a storyteller working at his peak.

—C.B. BERNARD
author of *Ordinary Bear*

The Divide is a thematically unified collection of stories, unflinchingly honest and unsentimental but packing an emotional wallop that's earned all the more for its dry-eyed depictions of lonely people struggling to find something to connect with in the world, in other people, and in themselves. In language that is lean, precise, and tactile, Williams creates worlds where everything is exactly as it is and nothing is as it seems. The stories are naturalistic, and yet in their heightened emotional tensions they sometimes push the boundaries of realism, intimating twilight worlds at the edge of consciousness. In this, his fourth book, Williams shows he is a storyteller at the height of his craft.

—JEFF FEARNSIDE
author of *Ships in the Desert*

The Divide is so much more than stories taking place in the Intermountain West adjacent to the Continental Divide. Its characters suffer rifts large and small, and personal slights, old memories, and the hot mess of relationships rise up like mountains, cold and hard. Williams' stories flow like a Rocky Mountain stream, in cool, clear prose.

—KEN POST
author of *Greyhound Cowboy*

THE DIVIDE

stories

Evan Morgan Williams

CORNERSTONE PRESS

UNIVERSITY OF WISCONSIN-STEVENS POINT

Cornerstone Press, Stevens Point, Wisconsin 54481
Copyright © 2026 Evan Morgan Williams
www.uwsp.edu/cornerstone

Printed in the United States of America.

Library of Congress Control Number: 2026930407
ISBN: 978-1-968148-27-0

Cornerstone Press titles are produced in courses and internships offered by the Department of English at the University of Wisconsin–Stevens Point.

DIRECTOR & PUBLISHER
Dr. Ross K. Tangedal

EXECUTIVE EDITORS
Jeff Snowbarger, Freesia McKee

EDITORIAL DIRECTOR
Brett Hill

SENIOR EDITORS
Paige Biever, Ellie Atkinson

PRESS STAFF
Samantha Bjork, Sophie McPherson, Madison Schultz, Autumn Vine, Lillian Kulbeck, Karlie Harpold, Eleanor Belcher, John Evans, McKenna Bartel, Ryleigh Miller

In memory of Chris Weaver

ALSO BY EVAN MORGAN WILLIAMS:

Stories of the New West

Canyons | Older Stories

Thorn

stories

And as for love—

why is it never enough
to save us?

—Erica Jong

Egg and Dart

The Egg and Dart opened for dinner at five o'clock, but no one came. The waiter stood in the doorway and let thirty minutes get away from him. He gazed at the empty avenue and wondered if he should flip the *Open* sign to *Closed*. He stepped into the sunshine. He was a large man, and he made his stance erect and strong, his spine tense, his hands anchored to his hips. You betcha.

His brother came out. He nudged past the waiter and said he was heading to the farmers' market for leeks. He said to keep it open. Said that Lois might drop by. In reply, the waiter mumbled about wasting Nana's leek soup recipe on a tramp like Lois, and he glared at his brother strolling down the sidewalk in his chef tunic, breezing past the vacant storefronts, whistling "So Much in Love" like a damn fool. The sun gleamed on the storefronts, the cracked windows, the peeling paint. The bony shadow of a streetlamp was the one dark thing. The chef leaped lightly over the shadow and was gone.

An empty streetcar whirred by.

A girl in a white dress walked up the sidewalk and sat at a table outside the Egg and Dart. This wasn't goddamned Lois. The waiter had seen this girl in the restaurant before and he had always liked her because she was pretty and nice, although *nice* meant that the waiter, with his blurry tattoos and scowl, didn't stand a chance with her. The girl shaded her eyes and peered down the street. Waiting for someone. The waiter shook his head sadly. A breeze caught the girl's dress, and she smoothed the wide skirt over her knees. She checked her watch. The waiter knew she had no money with her, she never had money, and if the evening got crowded, she couldn't hold the table. As if the Egg and Dart ever got crowded anymore! The girl flipped her watch and squinted at the back. Probably reading the inscription. From her mom and dad. Probably with love. The sunlight flashed off her hair.

A man came up the street, slid past the waiter, and took a table inside. He wore a brown rayon shirt. His hair was too long for a businessman; besides, the downtown offices had not let out. The man had taken a window table, and when the waiter came over, the man gave him a twenty to hold the table all night. The waiter did not mention that this was unnecessary, and he pocketed the twenty. The man set a rose on the table. The waiter put it in a vase. The man took out a jewelry store box and set it next to the vase. He ordered a bottle of Riesling and an hors d'oeuvre of smoked salmon with lemon and crushed sage. The waiter went into the kitchen and put together the dish as best he could. His brother had not returned. Goddamned Lois.

The waiter brought out the salmon and poured the man's wine. The man watched his wine being poured, then he looked at the pretty girl through the window. The girl was gazing down the street. She touched her hair. The waiter watched the man watching the girl, and he remarked that the girl was a regular at the Egg and Dart, and that she was waiting for a musician who sometimes played there. A two-chambered flute, or a drum with a soft buckskin mallet, a jingle wadded in his fist, his barrel voice warm and low.

"She thinks she's in love with him."

"Is her love in doubt?"

"It's more that she's too hopeful. Look: yoke collar and puffy sleeves. Morgan Fairchild hair. She's a goddamned dream girl."

"A what?"

"She deserves better than a musician, don't you think? A goddamned artiste. I happen to know he's going back to the rez." The waiter sighed and sat down at the man's table and filled the other glass for himself. He took a sniff of the cool white wine and breathed deeply. "The goddamned rez."

"Um, what are you doing?"

The waiter was a large man, and he fit only on the edge of the seat. His shadow sprawled across the table. "Don't worry. Indian hospitality. You won't forget this night, I tell you. You'll remember fondly: *the waiter, a strapping native buck, sat with us.* You'll tip me fine, and I won't forget this night either." They ate the smoked salmon and watched the pretty girl. The sunlight glowed through her dress and revealed the outline of her legs. The girl checked her watch again.

The man said, "I'm waiting for a date too."

"I know you're waiting for a date. You don't have to tell me you're waiting for a date." The waiter sniffed the wine again. He felt an edge. He would get a fat tip. You betcha.

The man said, "What else do you know?"

The waiter nodded at the flowers and the little box.

The man frowned and put the little box in his pocket. "What will she say?"

The waiter looked the man up and down. "Don't ask me that."

"That's not funny."

"Hey, don't blame me." The waiter held up his glass and looked at the sun through the pale wine. He reached for another slice of smoked salmon with lemon and sage. He gobbled this bite and took another. "These are delicious."

"Don't you have something to do? Before the rush?"

"I have time. Time is one thing Indian people have." He refilled the man's glass. He leaned closer, and the chair groaned from his shifting weight. "I mean, we have no time, really. A few months. The city wants us out. Everyone else on the block is already out. A few months. See, Indian people are always getting pushed out. But it only makes us care less about time."

They gazed thoughtfully into their glasses of wine. The waiter ran his thick finger around the rim of his glass, and the surface of the wine shimmered, but no tone came from the glass.

The man said, "So, uh, what tribe are you? What tribe is this place?"

"I'm from the human tribe. What tribe do I look like to you?"

"I just was wondering—"

"I was born in Warm Springs, in a little clinic that was really just a double-wide trailer, if that is the information you're looking for."

"So that would make you a Paiute, or maybe a Wasco."

"It would make me a fat, lonely, bitter man who has failed in love."

The girl glanced in the window at the two men, then looked away quickly.

The waiter said, "Look at her. She doesn't want me to go out there. If I do, she'll have to order something."

"I think it's romantic," the man said. "A pretty girl waiting for a musician. That's what I say."

"You can call it that."

"What do you call it?"

The waiter mumbled, "A goddamned shame."

"What did you say?"

The waiter cleared his voice. "Nothing."

The girl looked in the window at the man and smiled. The man looked back at her for a long time.

The waiter said, "That does it. I'm going out there." He set his wine glass on the table with a loud ping. He snatched up the man's bottle. There was a little slosh in the bottom. The man at the table watched his bottle of wine go away.

The waiter made flat, thudding steps, and the floor creaked as he walked out. He touched the girl, tugged on the puffy capped sleeve of her white dress. He set down a dry glass and poured the last of the man's wine. He stood beside her table. The girl rubbed her arms, but it wasn't cold. She looked in the window at the man with the rose and the engagement ring, and she smiled. She mouthed a thank you. The man nodded back.

The waiter exhaled and muttered, "Don't thank me, honey." He came back in and set the empty bottle on the man's table.

"She really is a pretty girl," the man said.

"She's a dream girl."

"Why do you keep saying that?"

"I said it only once before. No matter. She's a dream, meaning you can't have her. No one can have her. She's from Pendleton, but here she is in Portland, the big goddamned city, and she's going to be disappointed, and that tight waist and that lovely face and golden hair will be all she has."

"Maybe she's smart or she's a good cook. Maybe she's nice."

"Nice doesn't fill a dress just right."

"You're drunk." The man's jaw was setting tightly.

"No, I'm very disciplined about that. You need to be more observant. Have you seen me take a single sip? In fact, I am a friend of Bill. Here, you drink for me." He tipped the man's bottle, but it was empty.

The man said, "So tell me why the girl came to the city. Since you seem to know so much."

"Well, back home she has her parents who love her, but it's not enough. They've kept her bedroom exactly the same. The blue bedspread. The unicorn poster on the wall, but it's not enough. Me? I'm from the rez, but I have my brother here doing the cooking, so I tell myself I'm okay. But this girl, she chases a big-city dream, and it won't come true. You know, when you dream a good dream, you don't want it to end. You wake up, and it's so sad to find the dream gone. I tell you, I am a romantic, and I wish she would find a good man. But she won't."

"Because she's a dream girl."

"Oh, so you do understand."

"No."

"Listen. She has a mom and dad who love her. Maybe they gave her money for that dress. There's a boy back home. Maybe he gave her the watch and inscribed 'I love you' on the back in tiny letters. Maybe he's off in Desert Storm. She has that golden hair and that trim waist, but—"

"I don't know where she is."

"Who?"

"My date. My lady."

"She is coming, isn't she?"

"Why would you say that? Like it's in doubt? She's coming. There is no doubt, pal."

"No, I mean, of course she's coming. She wouldn't want to miss this, eh."

The man looked down. A private thought. He looked up and said, "So can you tell me the specials?"

"Let's wait for your date. Because she is coming—"

"Just tell me the damn specials."

"Well, there's salmon. That's all we have, really. I mean, we cook a ton of salmon. Smoked salmon. Grilled salmon. Salmon and chokecherry jam. Salmon fillet. Salmon steak. Pan-fried or on the grill. Poached salmon. I suppose I should mention we got commodity peanut butter too, commodity cheese, commodity canola oil…"

Outside the window, the dream girl finished her wine. She was standing with her arms folded sternly. She looked cold.

"I'm going to give her some more." The waiter took the bottle.

"No." The man grabbed the bottle.

The waiter pulled.

They both had forgotten it was empty.

"Your girl isn't even here yet."

"No."

"You're drinking alone on the night you propose to your beloved?"

"I'm drinking with you."

"You're drinking alone."

The shadow of the waiter was big and long across the table. The bottle came into his fat hand. "I'll get you a new one later. Be right back." The waiter set down the empty bottle and went out to the girl. He reached into his pocket and gave the girl some bills. She stood. She was crying. She held the money close, her hands near her throat, and she trudged down the sidewalk toward the streetcar stop. She walked past the stop and toward the bus stop on the next corner. The waiter came back inside and opened a new bottle.

"I'm sending her home."

"What did you give her?"

"A hundred dollars."

"Jesus. Do you want to fuck her?"

"Money to go home. If I wanted to fuck her, as I think we both do, I have a room upstairs for such purposes. And where is your date? This is supposed to be a romantic place."

"I don't know. She had a doctor's appointment, and she was going to meet me."

"Don't worry. She's coming. I'm sure of it. Do you want some more food?"

"I don't know."

"To go with the wine. I'm giving you more wine, you know."

"Maybe something."

"More salmon. On the house, because, I mean, we got lots of salmon. Got so much salmon…"

"But there's no cook. Where is the cook?"

"More wine then." He reached over with the new bottle and poured noisily. Drops splashed on the table. "There's this tramp named Lois, you see, and the cook, well, he…"

The shadows of the vacant storefronts grew long. The shade had reached the sidewalk tables now. The waiter cleared the girl's empty glass. For an hour, the waiter sat with the man as the man drank wine. The waiter led him down the wine list. Local stuff. Yamhill River. Rogue Valley. Columbia Gorge. He thought about cracking his trusty Night Train joke, but this wasn't the right guy. The waiter told the man about the crowds that used to come to the Egg and Dart. Men in loose silk shirts and women in high heels used to float out of Mercedes and BMW coupes. The sidewalk tables were always too cold for the women in their little sheath dresses, and the restaurant became a box of noise and sweat and perfume. People drank wine as fast as he could pour. His brother cooked salmon steaks on the grill and served them up with cornbread and plates of grilled squash and Nana's gooseberry jam. Then the waiter rolled out the drum and buckskin mallets, and drunken white men drifted out to the sidewalk and sang victory songs from a rez where they had never been. Very much later, after the fancy people were gone, the Indian folk in flannel shirts and Army coats came off the streets and sang the good songs and told the good stories, and the waiter and his brother always brought out the best recipes—soups, squash, sage honey, cowboy coffee with the grounds swimming in the bottom of the mug. At such times, he could pull off that Night Train joke pretty good, you betcha. In the morning, the waiter and his brother sent the Indian folk away, with take-out boxes of good, greasy salmon in their hands.

The man in the rayon shirt asked, with a slurred voice, "So how did this place get its name? The Egg and Dart. Some kind of Indian thing?"

"Look at that." The waiter pointed at the crown molding below the ceiling. "That's called *egg and dart*. That's where we got the name. Neo-classical, I guess, whatever that means. And do you see them cracks from the '93 quake? The city says shut us down. They want condos or rowhouses or something.

I say someone's on the take. I'm not on the take. I wish I was on the take. No Indian ever been on the goddamned take."

"So, will you bring out the drum for us?"

"No." The waiter held up his hand. "Maybe. I don't know. Listen, maybe your girl is caught in traffic. She'll be really late. In a way, it will make your night more meaningful. Like it came close to not happening, but then it did. Tell you what: if she shows, I'll bring out the drum."

"This was my fiancé's favorite restaurant when she taught at Reed. She's always telling me about it. But I don't come into the city much. I teach at Linfield and—"

"You're lucky to get a table. Not because of the crowd, obviously." The waiter laughed. He threw a cork at the egg and dart molding, and it bounced around the empty restaurant. "Goddamned inspectors. By the way, she's not your fiancé yet."

The man's jaw set up firm again. "You said I would never forget this night. You were right: you're spoiling everything."

"Take it easy, brother."

"I'm just pissed. I'm pissed at you, and I'm pissed at her."

A couple came in. The man wore a silk shirt, and the woman had a dress in the latest style, short and loose, a shift. She had black bobbed hair.

"The chef's not back," said the waiter.

"What?"

The man who was waiting for his date spoke up. "No chef tonight. Something to do with a certain Lois. So we're drinking. We're drinking and fighting."

"Indian hospitality," shrugged the waiter. He and the man laughed.

The man in the silk shirt said, "This used to be a good place." He and the girl sulked out. The door swung shut.

The waiter stood up and flipped a switch on the wall. The lights went down.

"We're closing now."

"What? You can't. Wait. No."

The waiter stood by the table. He took the man's water glass and drank it down. He drank down his own. He picked up the man's wine glass, thought about it, then set it down. He said, "Listen to me. You and your girl should not marry. Calm the fuck down and listen to me. Consider the evidence. One, you were staring at that dream girl, which your fiancé could not have known about, of course, but, as you are so wandering of the eye, your 'fiancé,' as you call her, has already sensed it numerous times before, so what is the point of her coming? Two: you have eaten my smoked salmon and chokecherry jam, and you've drunk wine without her; you are maybe even glad she was not here, as it meant more food and wine for you. Three: there is a reason she is not coming to her special dinner: you said she had a medical appointment. It is not so hard to see what this means. She's sobbing in her car. She got bad news. Cancer. Lupus. I don't know. Something bad. But she's not seeking you out in her moment of need. She can't bear to even start the motor. How do I know this? How do you NOT know? You don't even wonder about it."

"Well…"

"There's one more thing. Listen to me. You're mad at your girl, or so you say, but deeply you're glad about being mad because it allows you to feel something. Because otherwise," the waiter paused, loving this part, fists grinding on the table, "you don't feel anything."

"Fuck you."

"No feeling. None. What do you teach, political science, or something?"

"Come off it. We were drinking wine. We were having a good time."

"She will turn to someone she trusts, and she wants it to be you, but she knows it isn't you. Now, if you will excuse me," he flipped the sign to *Closed*, "If you hurry, maybe you can catch the pretty girl in the white dress. She really doesn't know the buses very well, see, and—"

"You fat prick." The man stood, lunged for the waiter, and stumbled. He grabbed onto the table for balance. The table tipped. The water glasses and wine glasses and empty bottles slid and crashed. The waiter caught the man and held him as the table went over. His big hands held the man's arms. He imagined it was possible to hold in his heart all the man's pain, but there was only his own pain, and his stories, all his good stories, and here was just a man in his arms.

He said, "A man got to feel something."

"I'll kick your ass."

"Why don't you come upstairs and sleep it off. I know how it is. I know this. I goddamn know what it means to feel."

"I said I'll kick your ass. I promise that I will." The man gave in to the waiter's strong arms.

"Come on. I know." The waiter and the man were dark shapes in the restaurant.

"She might come." The man was out of breath.

"I'll be here for her if she does. She can tell her story to me. There's plenty of wine, plenty of salmon. You already know what a good listener I am. So come along. That's it now. There's a couch and blankets upstairs. There's the egg and dart molding too. All the walls have egg and dart. You can run your fingers across it. Feel the cracks. Feel all the perfect solid places, too. Feel where they start and feel where they end."

The Clear Blue Sky

They always remembered how cold it was. It was the one story they could tell together, husband and wife, laughing as they completed each other's sentences: how cold it was. How the sun dropped behind the Tetons early and left the sky so blank and blue. And cold. Good thing they had each other to keep warm. On the patio behind the tavern, Paul and Emily danced in each other's arms. The piano, a weathered upright, stood unused against the wall. Paul and Emily were alone. They danced in the cold.

Grit rolled beneath Paul's soles. Flecks of yellow granite crumbled into powder beneath his heel. Emily, wearing a blouse too thin for cold, too city-slicker for Jackson Hole, pressed close to him. They danced to keep their bodies warm.

The waitress, probably a college girl on a summer job—because that's how it always was in Jackson Hole—came out to wipe the tables. Her hair was loose, and it got in the way of her work, and she flipped it back, but the breeze came up, and her hair got in her face again. The girl's breath made a cloud that vanished quickly in the dry air. Paul watched her. Emily was watching too. The girl closed the piano lid and draped a tarp over it, and the tarp rustled in the breeze, and Paul and Emily danced to no music, but they had been doing that for a long time.

"So, Paul..." Emily said.

Paul gazed at her eyes. Her beautiful blue eyes.

She said, "Do you remember our first dance? I'm asking you. The first time. Do you remember?"

Paul did not answer. Emily hummed a tune. Paul did not know it.

"Well? Do you remember?"

"I remember it was cold."

"What else do you remember?"

He remembered all of it. He said, "How do I answer that?"

"You tell the truth. You tell the truth to your woman, whom you love."

"Listen, you remember as well as I do, and that should be enough. I have you here now, and that's what matters."

She said, "Of course you don't want to talk about it. And, yes, I do remember. We danced for just one song, and then I played the piano for you and Kimberly. And you danced with her, not with me, the rest of the night. It was her last night of the summer. I drove her to the Trailways depot the very next day."

"Well, I don't want to reminisce right now."

"I do. I remember. My hands were cold, and I was the girl alone. Kimberly was dancing with you. You're the one who set her off on that ballroom dancing a jig. That's how it was."

"Do you tell me this to wound?"

"Ah, so it hurts."

"No, not really."

"Ah, so you're a tough guy now."

"No."

"I played that very piano right over there, and you danced with her. The middle C has a broken key. Did you know it was my print dress she wore? She wore it better, anyway. Too girly for me. I gave it to her. She hugged you in my dress. Do you know what it's like to watch that? Everyone else was watching too. We were all tired, ready to go back to the condo and flop, and we were cold, but Kimberly didn't want you to leave. She wanted you to dance for so long. She loved you. She wanted to fuck you, Paul. She loved you so. She has probably wondered ever since about you and her. It was a time she needed you to love her, and you didn't. Don't you wonder about that time? You can tell me, Paul, ten years out. Don't lie to yourself, you do wonder about it."

Paul gazed at her blue eyes. He did not say, "What makes you think she and I didn't fuck?" Instead, he said, "I thought this was supposed to be our story."

"Oh, it's definitely our story, Paul."

"Then it's already known, right? We can stop telling it right now."

Emily said, "We should get someone to play." She turned to the college girl. "Excuse me. Can you play that thing?"

The girl shook her head. The piano was already tucked beneath its tarp where it belonged. The girl was blowing out candles on the tables. Most of the candles had already died in the breeze. The girl flipped back her hair.

Paul said, "I remember that you played something by Cole Porter, right?"

Emily said, "*Begin the Beguine*, honey."

"Okay…"

"One hundred and eight bars without a repeat."

"I'll take your word for that."

They danced. His lips touched her warm hair. He said, "I remember she was always late for her shift." Paul felt Emily's shoulders tighten. He said, "She would hurry up the steps to the patio and tie her apron, and she would turn, her skirt swinging around, and her hair swinging around. She'd say in her accent, 'Do I look all right?' And she smelled like peppermint. Her hair smelled like goddamn peppermint."

"You must have been very close to her to smell her shampoo. What else do you remember? I've never heard this tidbit before."

Paul looked at the college girl picking up the salt-and-pepper shakers and putting them on a tray. The girl might have been singing. Paul thought he heard music. The girl was young and pretty. He did not say, "I remember feeling stunned at the perfection of my life." He said nothing.

Emily said, "Well, I remember something. The owner gave her the best tables, and the patrons gave her the best tips and followed her with their eyes. You don't remember that, do you? You wouldn't, stuck in the kitchen."

"Sounds like a girl thing to remember."

"And what if Kimberly and you had stayed together, Paul? Do you ever wonder about that? Or is that a girl thing too?"

"I don't think about that."

"The hell you don't."

"Okay. Maybe she and I would have been like you and me."

"So, you do think about it."

"No."

"We're interchangeable. We're just women."

"Jesus Christ."

"You could have had that life, Paul, but instead you have this life, with me, and that other hypothetical life feels warm and alive, while this life brings you pain sprung simply from the fact that this life is not that other one. The grass is always greener. So you see what you and I have to look back on, Paul: I was not your one true love. We had summer jobs in Jackson Hole. I can say that much. I wore an apron and kept my hair loose and smelling like peppermint too. But you don't remember me. I played the piano while Kimberly and you danced the fucking night away."

"Jesus Christ, Emily."

And they danced. Paul spun Emily around.

There were no more tables to clean, and the college girl sat by the light and read from a thick book and waited for Paul and Emily to leave. She probably didn't care. The longer they stayed, the more she would be paid. She drew herself a sparkling water. She put on a thick cardigan and wrapped it close.

The sky turned deeper blue, and the blue was broken up by the first stars.

Emily said, "I don't get that. Night comes so early here."

"It's the Tetons blocking out the setting sun. Everything's in shadow now. The evening has a long way to go, but we don't have the direct sun anymore."

"I still don't get that. I didn't like it then or now. It's always too cold."

"Well, that's a difference between me and you. Welcome to the Rockies."

"Don't go looking for differences. You actually seem to like looking for differences. Do you suppose we're even dancing to the same song, Paul?"

And they danced. Paul dipped Emily, then brought her up.

She looked at him. Blue eyes. She said, "Why didn't you love her when you had the chance?"

"Jesus Christ."

"Why, Paul?"

"I did love her."

"I knew it!"

"But…"

"But what?"

"I don't know."

"I do know, Paul. I stole you away."

"No, you didn't."

"I stole you, didn't I? I wanted you more. You were too nice to hurt me by saying so. She was too nice, too. So why don't you say that now? All three of us would be happier. She went back to England, then I stole you away."

"No."

"Say it."

"No. That's not it at all."

"So, what is it?"

"I don't know."

And they danced.

"Be a man."

"This is being a man."

"That's what you have to tell yourself now that you're stuck with me." Emily began to cry. Her familiar warmth. Her familiar tears. Paul could smell them on the front of his shirt.

"Stuck with you? You're not exactly making a strong case for yourself."

"I don't have to make a case for myself. I have you now and forever, and I'm so god damned happy."

"I'm just saying that you were the right one and that's why it's worked out."

"But Paul, you're not supposed to have feelings for anyone but me. Just by saying I'm the right one and it's worked out, that isn't enough. Big deal. Gee, I'm so glad to know that I 'worked out' for you. That's so romantic, Paul."

There was no music. Paul wanted to sit down.

"She loved you. She still loves you." Emily wiped her eyes. "This was a total mistake to come back here. I want to go home."

Paul said, "We are home."

And they danced. Paul thought about the aspens turning late-summer yellow, the older ones being the first to turn. He said, "We were twenty-two, and we—"

"I just want to know one thing. Why me?"

"You already know. You've always known."

"I want to hear it again."

Paul thought about this. He said, "Once upon a time, there was the clear blue sky. Around four o'clock, the sun dropped behind the western mountains, and the deep shade caught us by surprise. We should have known. And with the shade came the cold. We should have known that, too. We were the only ones on the patio anymore. Kimberly had gone back to England by then. The rest of the gang had gone back to school. My arms held you close. There was music, and I didn't see how time could end, although this was summer in the Rockies, where the ending was, by late August, clearly on its way, if one chose to notice the cold on one's skin, the change in the flicker's call, the drift in the edges of the aspen leaves from green to gold. You remember how it was. We didn't want to leave, but to stay past August was like watching time fly away."

Paul heard the grit beneath his hard heels. This was not music. They were not dancing. He was grinding grit. Happily ever after.

The girl read her thick book and drank her water, and it was almost gone.

Emily said, "That makes absolutely no fucking sense, Paul."

The air was cold. The night was cold. It was all cold. They had forgotten the cold. They had forgotten hating this town, Jackson Hole, wearing their thin city clothes and being so cold. Keep dancing. In the cold. On the cold granite stones. To no music. Emily will tug against you. She will hold on. It's not about the past anymore, it's you and your wife, on the latest battleground, the latest way you don't understand each other, the latest way you don't fit each other's dreams, the latest way you aren't living happily ever after.

The college girl set down her big book. She was watching them.

Paul thought, *She has no idea.*

The girl said, "Excuse me. I have to close now. Sorry. I really have to go home."

Paul said, "That's all right."

"It's just that I'm on a bike, and it gets so dark so early."

"It certainly does."

The girl said, "So are you guys like, in love, or something?"

Emily said, "Oh yes. In love, or something. That's exactly what we are."

Paul said, "Some name for a bar. 'The Clear Blue Sky.' I always thought so."

The girl said, "At least it's hopeful. It has a hopeful ring to it."

Paul said, "Of course you have to say that."

The waitress buttoned her sweater and went inside. The patio lights went down.

Emily whispered, "That wasn't nice." She leaned in tighter.

He said, "Sorry."

Emily said, "'Sorry' does it?"

"Of course it does."

Paul and Emily finished their dance. They twirled. His knees had become sore from dancing on the hard stone.

Emily whispered, "Say her name."

"What? The waitress?"

"Say Kimberly's name."

"I'm not saying her name."

"That's better."

"We need to leave, Emily."

"Where should we go, Paul? I mean, where did you and she go when you—"

"I don't suppose it really matters, does it?"

"Where did you do it?"

He did not say anything.

"Come on. Jackson's a small town. Everyone knows a good place. I'll go in and ask the girl…" She pulled away.

"No, you won't." Paul took Emily's wrist. She let him pull her in. He held her close and said, "Listen. She and I never did it. Never went anywhere. But let's go to the high rocks over the Snake. That would be a good place. It may be cold, but the rocks will still be warm."

"All right. Let's go there. You know the way?" She wasn't crying now. Her beautiful eyes.

"I think I remember the way. I'll take you to my spot."

"Our spot."

"Sure."

They went inside to pay their tab. The girl had locked the register. She unlocked it for them.

"Good night," said Paul.

"Good night," said the girl.

Paul watched the girl watching them go.

Down the Mountain

The climbers rested on the col and undid the ropes that linked them together. The south ridge descended sharp and steep, blinding white in the sun. Compared to the sheer ice face they had come down, the ridge would be easy going. Everyone was glad to take off their harnesses and ropes.

Mark let the weight fall from his hips. His hips felt sweaty where the harness had rubbed, and the damp spots on his clothes felt pleasantly cool in the sub-zero air. He and the other guide were already in T-shirts. The Japanese climbers were less willing to strip down, but Mark knew they would shed their fancy red parkas soon enough. The climb down the south ridge would be a haul.

Most of the climbers drifted to the edge of the col and examined the Seward Glacier far below. Beyond the glacier rose the front range of the St. Elias mountains and, on the horizon, the Pacific Ocean. Mark didn't bother. He'd seen it too many times. He coiled the ropes.

The lone woman in the party also stayed back from the edge. She was kneeling on the ice, her back to the men. She had removed her gloves, and she was writing in a journal in Japanese characters. Her helmet was off, and her bobbed black hair slid across her face.

Mark thought he ought to say something to her, like how pretty she looked, but he tied off the coils of rope and said nothing.

The other guide hoisted his backpack onto his shoulders and warned the Japanese climbers not to leave anything behind, because damned if he was coming back for anyone's camera. Nobody laughed. It was a stupid joke. But he was right, Mark thought: Get off this beast. Good weather wouldn't last forever. Get it while you can.

Crunch of crampons, ping of ice axes, dull clink of ice screws and carabiners dangling from backpacks. Earlier that day, they had traversed a bad ice wall, rotten and crumbly, and maybe these clients hadn't been ready, and maybe the other guide had been right to protest, but Mark had led them across anyway. No one had gotten hurt. They had been lucky. Mark wanted it behind him now, and he began the long slog down the ridge. The woman hoisted her pack and followed him, and the rest of the party fell in behind.

It was work. The snow was a mush Mark sank into as deep as his hips. By one o'clock, he had drained his water bag. He let his body fall forward with each step, and he kept his legs moving. Let gravity do the work. The straps pulled at his shoulders. A few more hours, and he would dump ropes and ice gear at the warming hut. There would be the chopper ride to Kluane Lake. Hot tubs and margaritas at the lodge by midnight. No one would remember the bad ice wall. They would only remember the summit—glimmering, icy, bright, blue, cold, spectacular.

Mark absent-mindedly sucked on the spigot of his water bag, but he got nothing.

Keep moving down. Don't get separated too far. Stay in each other's sight. No talking. All good.

Mark turned and looked back up the ridge. The woman had stopped to pee. She wouldn't pee if Mark was watching, so he faced down the ridge. He flexed his arms. After three days of thick, steamy clothes, he was glad to see his own skin.

The woman caught up to him, and they walked together. "The ice wall…"

"What about it?"

"We hear it pop-pop."

"We were late. The ice was soft."

"Because of the danger, we could sleep above it for another night and climb down tomorrow early. I mean in the cold."

"Looking back, I suppose…"

"You did not want to spend another night?"

"We made out all right."

Mark let the woman go ahead. He didn't want to talk. He looked back. The distance between the climbers was growing, each in his own thoughts as they descended the ridge. Farthest in back, the other guide waved him on. All good. Mark resumed walking. There were times when you had to be a team, but this was not one, and Mark was glad to be alone and watching the Japanese woman move down the mountain. He did not like talking. Thinking of talking was better than talking. *Don't talk.* He'd said that before. With the right girl, just being near each other all day was enough, and Mark could talk to her in his thoughts and know by the way she turned to him in the evening, brushing arms, meeting his gaze, that she had been talking to him in her thoughts too. The Japanese woman had been like that. Her Japanese phrases had not worked into English right, but she and Mark hadn't needed talking. It had happened last night. They had shared a tent, and he and the girl had not talked.

He caught up with her and adjusted some ice screws that were dangling from her pack. He turned the woman toward him and kissed her. Maybe there would be another night? From the kiss, he couldn't tell. Not being able to tell was a bad sign.

The sun was bright. The woman had stripped to a tight Polartec undershirt, and she had not put her helmet back on. After three days of thick parka and gloves and helmet and impenetrable dark glasses, she looked graceful and sexy.

All that clothing, all that cold: above fifteen thousand feet you measured every motion. Every zipper, every snap, every drawstring, every clip. Even breathing, at fifteen thousand feet, was measured, even fucking was measured and tight and hard. Now Mark could see her shoulders and slender arms and narrow waist and her smooth hair along the line of her jaw. She was small—her ice axe and backpack and boots were sized for a child—and Mark had figured her for about twenty, but the other guide had said she was in medical school. Mark had looked into medical school, but he had dropped out of college his senior year, taken the guide job, and never gone back. Never did pay his student loans.

By four o'clock, the temperature fell below freezing, and the snow hardened. The wind came up. They made better time. Long steps. Solid crunchy ice. Crampons biting and holding. Mark could go forever like this, but at the bottom of the ridge lay another col, flat and low, and the warming hut with the orange-painted zinc roof. The edge of the Seward Glacier lapped at the col, smooth and wide and flat as the sea.

Mark and the woman reached the hut. The rest of the party was way back.

The door caught a gust of wind and swung away from Mark. It was a small doorway, and Mark had to stoop to get through, but it was easy for the woman. A change in the swirling wind, and the door closed behind them with a slam. The passage had a metal grate floor, and they took off their crampons, hung up their ice axes, and hung the ropes carefully away from the axes.

The main room was dark and smelled of port wine, tobacco, and Coleman fuel. The zinc roof rattled. Along the walls lay wooden benches with climbers sprawled out, unfamiliar shapes in their thick parkas, waiting for their chopper down. No, they were preparing to go up. That's why they weren't talking. Nervous. Maybe it was the port wine. Some of them looked up as Mark and the woman entered.

A climber Mark recognized, Bernice, was guiding the party. She waved from where she sat against the far wall.

Mark and the woman found a bench and sat. The woman bent over her pack, and her shiny, smooth hair fell forward. She took off her sweat-stained Polartec, and she pulled a fresh sweater out of her pack. She wasn't wearing a bra, not that she needed one, and the bones of her spine curved in a smooth line. Mark wanted to touch her, but she was turned away. On a climb, you weren't supposed to care about seeing each other naked. Hell, last night, they had been all over each other. Maybe this modesty was a Japanese thing.

She smoothed the sweater down.

They took turns kneeling, and with a bristle brush they scrubbed the ice crystals out of each other's boot laces and seams. On his turn, Mark looked up. She was looking directly at him, but he could not read her eyes. Not like last night. He could read her eyes then. Now her head was tilted, and he wanted to tuck her hair back from her face.

Mark sat with the woman in the big room and said nothing. They propped their feet on their packs. His pack was worn, hers was new. Mark wondered if she'd ever need it again. The woman's head was down. She was leaning forward and fidgeting with her boots, but Mark had just cleaned them, and he knew they were fine.

"Can I talk to you?" he said. He hated this. He hated this part.

"You are talking to me now."

"Outside? Away from all this?"

"Who will watch my pack?"

"Nobody wants your stuff."

"That is not true. A thief stole my wallet in Vancouver."

"Come on."

The woman followed Mark outside. It was still bright, but now it had become cold. They stood in the sun. Mark guessed it was five o'clock.

"If a thief takes my stuff..."

"You don't need your stuff."

"My journal!" The woman gasped. "I left my journal up there!" She brought her hands to her face. Her new sweater was white and soft and tight to her skin.

"Listen, this doesn't have to be the end for us. You have a few more days. We could—"

"My journal!"

The woman ran back inside. Mark followed. He sat beside her while she rummaged through her pack, but what could he do?

Bernice shuffled over to their bench. She held a bottle and two paper cups. She sat on the other side of Mark and smiled.

"You guys want some port? We got more bottles." She poured two Dixie cups of port and handed them to Mark, and he gave one to the woman. She was straining her face not to cry, but Mark could see tears.

"Looks like you kicked ass on the north spur," Bernice said. She elbowed Mark. "Looks like you got some ass too."

"I guess."

"Did you hear on the radio?"

"What?"

"Davey's party had a slip on the ice wall. Someone went down. They've radioed for a stretcher."

"That's something." Mark wanted to change the subject. Too close for comfort. "Um, this is Tomoko. We came down from the col. Poor Tomoko has lost her journal—"

"And doesn't know where to find it!" Bernice made a goofy smile but then stopped. "I'm Bernice, by the way."

"Nice to meet you," Tomoko said. "I am sorry to cry. My journal is so important to me."

"Tomoko's a medical student from Japan."

"Oh?"

"I am graduated. No more school. Doctor."

"And you guys are friends, obviously."

"Yes. I mean, we've become friends."

"Friends? It's good that you've become friends. It's very good. It's good because—"

"Bernice!" Mark hated all this talking.

Tomoko looked at her cup of port. Bernice got up and walked the bottle around the room.

Mark said, "She's an old friend." It sounded a little desperate.

"I see." Tomoko held the cup of port to her mouth.

"It's not like that." Mark had swallowed his.

"What is it not like?"

"Nothing, really. We're friends."

"Nothing? Just as bad as something."

The door opened and the rest of Mark's party bustled in. They were hot, and they were tired. The room stank of sweat. More port. Japanese voices, noisy and triumphant. Mark was relieved. The ice wall would make a good story. So why did he feel sad? Why did he look at Tomoko's face and hair and tight white sweater and narrow waist and feel sad? They had been naked, fifteen thousand feet, thirty below zero, but it was not dangerous as long as nothing went wrong, and nothing had! Nothing ever went wrong with fucking. But when it was over and they had thickened their layers and slid into their bags, Mark couldn't tell: was she crying? Her sleeping bag became a lumped shape, and the bag glowed from her flashlight. What was she doing in that sleeping bag? Writing in her journal? That's what she was doing!

"When do you have to get back to school?"

"I already tell you. I am done with school. I work in a trauma center."

Tomoko wrapped a bandana around her hair and tied it at the back of her neck. Mark watched her spine bending forward. He noticed, for the first time, a tattoo where her sweater lifted. It wasn't fine work. A flower. He could tell that much. Dark skin.

"Where'd you get the tat?"

"Africa." She pulled the hem of her sweater down.

"You've been around."

"No, I have not."

"That's not what I meant."

"Excuse me?"

"Nothing. You've been to a lot of places, that's all."

"I made an internship with Medicine Sans Frontier." She shifted, leaving a space between them. "The tattoo, my friend and I got one. We were foolish." Tomoko took a sip of her port and looked at the dark red liquid. A drop spilled onto her hand, and she kissed it off. Her lips quivered. "Listen, I do not usually do this kind of thing."

Another bottle was coming around, and Mark topped off both their cups. They sat in the hut and drank the port.

Tomoko set her cup down. "I do not like this strong wine. And I did not like last night very much. But I like you." Her eyes were tearing again.

"I liked it. I liked you. You're a damn sweet girl."

"What happens now?"

"Anything we want."

"We?"

"There's still a *we*."

"Still? So *we* is a fragile thing?"

"It ends eventually. All my *we's* end. But—"

"All your *we's*?"

"You're not the first." His voice was louder than he had meant, and he knew he sounded defensive. He didn't want this talking.

"Mark, I do not do this."

"That's all right."

"I do not know why I—"

"It's all right."

"You think I am a fool. You probably do this every climb. I am just a fool." She wasn't crying anymore.

"Um, you've really never fucked before, have you?"

The word shook her. She winced.

"Yes, I have too."

"Then you should know it's not a big deal."

She looked down. "I have fucked before. Do you think I am a silly schoolgirl? But—I am thinking of the right word—I regretted that time, and I regret this time too."

"I'm sorry." Mark was cross. Was it the port or the anger that warmed his skin?

Tomoko said, "You should not be sorry. That proves you think it was a regretting thing too."

The roof of the warming hut began to shudder. A chopper had come in. An emergency crew bustled into the hut: four rangers wearing Park Service orange jackets and helmets. Radio squawking. They carried an empty stretcher-toboggan, and they laid it on the metal grate floor.

"What are they doing here?" Tomoko said.

"There was an accident on the ice wall. They're going up. The chopper can't go any higher than this."

Tomoko said, "I should go too."

"But you're just—"

"I am a doctor in the trauma specialty. I should go." Tomoko started getting into her parka.

"If this is about your journal—"

"I can look after myself. More than you know." Tomoko was busy with her backpack.

"Look, don't be sore. We can still hang out at the lodge."

"Right. And you can come to Japan, and I will show to you the mountains."

"Yeah, I could blow this scene for a while. I could bum Japan."

"You can stay at my apartment and meet my mother and father."

"Sure."

"No."

"It's nice to talk about, don't you think?"

"Not at all."

"But—"

"We can please stop talking?"

Tomoko walked over to the rangers and began talking to them. Mark crumpled his paper cup. He watched her start to bow to the rangers, then stop the bow to shake their hands. The rangers looked huge next to her. She sure as hell didn't look like a doctor. The rangers and Tomoko continued talking.

Bernice came over and leaned against Mark's side. She gazed at him sleepily. Too much port. She would be all right.

"You going down, hon'?" she said.

"Yeah. You come with me if you like. There's a party at the lodge. My clients paid for a suite. Japanese. Fucking loaded."

"We're going up, dummy, not down. Anyway, you already got yours."

"You're drunk," Mark said. "And never mind me."

Mark watched Tomoko across the room. The rangers wore serious faces. Tomoko was nodding at their information. Then she became the giver of information, and the rangers did the nodding. Then they were all talking at once, talking about the same things at the same time. Tomoko's hair slipped out of her bandana, and she reached to tuck it back. Mark looked down and clenched his jaw. *We can talk about this!* He almost said it out loud.

Mark gathered his things and went out to the chopper, then remembered it wasn't his turn. It wasn't his chopper. He was going down. He looked back into the dark of the hut for Tomoko, but he couldn't see her. Talk about nothing.

The Stick Up

Hannah took her baby for a stroll. They went to story time at the library, and after story time, they headed to the cafe. This meant passing the sewer repair, where the men paused their work to watch Hannah walk by. Hannah walked briskly, the wheels on her stroller rattling. As she neared the cafe, she saw a girl out front, one hand on a stroller, the other gripping a cellphone. Hannah recognized her from story time: Lyudmila, a nanny. She was speaking Russian on her phone, sweetly at first, then harshly, then sweetly again. Hannah stepped up to her. Lyudmila set down her phone and eyed Hannah. She said hello. Hannah smiled and said hello. Lyudmila was pretty and young, and Hannah invited her for a cup. These girls never had money. It would be Hannah's treat. Later, they could walk together past the sewer crew. Strength in numbers. Hannah waited for Lyudmila to answer. Lyudmila said nothing, studying Hannah with sharp blue eyes. Hannah fidgeted with the handle of her stroller. Just as Hannah felt humiliated and regretful and ready to say, "Maybe another time," Lyudmila smiled tightly and said, "Okay."

Hannah and Lyudmila pushed their strollers inside and stood in line. Hannah was startled when Lyudmila took her hand and held it. Hannah pulled back at first, but Lyudmila's hand felt smooth and warm. Lyudmila raised

Hannah's hand and examined her wedding ring, a single large diamond on a platinum band. "Cool," she said. She lowered Hannah's hand, but she continued to hold it. Hannah smiled at the novelty of holding hands.

Hannah ordered two vanilla lattes while Lyudmila pushed the strollers to a table. The lattes came across the counter in thick porcelain mugs. The barista smiled at Hannah and said, "Your daughter is so pretty," nodding toward Lyudmila. Hannah carried the mugs to the table. She was smirking at the barista's remark. She sat down and unbuckled her baby from the stroller. She twisted her wedding ring off and set it in the cupholder of the stroller, and she lifted her baby girl. She pressed her cheek against the baby's warm, soft hair. Lyudmila watched her.

"It's so I don't scratch her."

"What?"

"The ring. Off."

"What? I don't—"

Lyudmila's cellphone beeped. Lyudmila read the message, masking her smile with her fingers.

Hannah said, "Are you in love, Lyudmila?"

"Lyuda. If you say Lyudmila, it is not personal." She had a trace of an accent. Mostly, she sounded like an American girl.

"Lyuda, then. Are you in love?"

Lyuda reached down and stroked the cheek of the baby in her stroller. "With this little angel? I'm crazy for him. I want to keep him. There's no way you can understand." She gazed at the baby. The baby gazed at her.

"I mean are you in love romantically?"

Lyuda looked at Hannah. Too long. She said, "I can tell you anything. I can say yes, no, anything, and you can't tell difference."

It had not occurred to Hannah that they would lie to each other. Why would they do that? She said, "You can't lie about being in love. That was your boyfriend on the phone, wasn't it? Were you speaking Russian?"

"It was Ukrainian, but it's same as Russian. I mean, it's not really same, but you can call them same if you want."

"What did you tell him?"

"I told him to be nice to me always. You have to say it, you know."

"I suppose that's true. I mean, I don't think I've ever said it, but it's certainly not a bad idea to say such a thing from time to time."

"Why? Your husband, he isn't nice to you?"

"Keith's always nice to me. He's very nice."

"Look at this," Lyuda leaned forward and showed Hannah her pendant, a blue sapphire set in silver against her pale skin. She hooked it with her finger. "This is a present. Boys have to be nice to me. I demand it." Her bright blue eyes narrowed. "What about you? Are you in love—because you just said you can't lie about love."

"Of course I'm in love." Hannah said. "But Keith and I get so busy. I don't really have time to think about love."

"Well, I have time to think about it. And I am in love." Lyuda leaned down and kissed the sleeping baby boy.

Hannah said, "You'll see, someday. You'll have to think practically. I'm not saying it's right, but love takes a back seat. I mean, it becomes, well, you'll be so busy. You'll see."

"Busy? So you are not making love with, what is his name, with Keith?" Lyuda reached for her latte. "You don't seem very busy to me." She took a sip. "Thanks for this beverage, by the way."

Hannah lifted her own mug. It was thick and heavy. She did not answer the question about not sleeping with Keith, but she was glad the girl had asked, and she let the question exist, a fact that had happened between them, like the two of them holding hands.

Lyuda's eyes were pools of blue. She said, "Come on. Tell me. We are two girls talking close now. You know, sharing stuff."

Hannah decided to play along. "Well, if you must know, Keith and I do sleep together. Not like we used to, though. When you're older and more practical, that will make sense to you."

"You are not so old."

"The barista thought I was your mom."

Lyuda laughed.

Hannah's hair was frosted and cut in a smooth bob. She wore a Lycra track suit—the suit showed off her trim figure. The pregnancy had deepened her voice, and she tolerated being mistaken for an older woman because it meant she was taken seriously. At the construction site, she still got the admiring stares from the men, but not the whistles anymore. Hannah would continue to look thirtysomething, angular and serious and smooth and happy, for a long time.

Hannah sipped her latte and watched Lyuda, who wore no makeup but looked lovely. Lyuda's eyes seemed to conduct a long study of Hannah's face.

Lyuda said, "In fact, you do not look like my mom at all. No wrinkles, no fat."

Hannah said, "Come on. The really sick thing is that you look only fifteen."

Lyuda's blonde hair was twisted into a loose bun, and she wore jeans and a blue hooded sweater. She said, "Boys like me the way I am. Boys stop me on sidewalk and tell me so."

"They flatter you because you're off-limits. Because you look fifteen. Because you look too pretty. Because you're pushing a stroller. Because you're Russian. Ukrainian. Whatever. You're off-limits. And they're called men, not boys."

Lyuda said, "I am not off-limits." She fingered her sapphire pendant.

"It's perception. They flatter me too, but it's because I'm claimed." She held out her hand to flash the diamond, but she remembered it was in the cupholder. She closed her hand. She wondered if Lyuda understood anything. Perception. Flatter. Claimed.

Lyuda finished off her latte, leaned forward, and asked Hannah, "Do you mind if I hold her?"

"Of course you can hold her!" Hannah leaned close, her knees touching Lyuda's knees, and she shifted her baby girl to Lyuda's arms. Lyuda cradled the baby and gazed into her eyes. The baby gazed back peacefully.

"She likes stories. I don't know if she understands the words, but she likes them. You could tell her a story. In Ukrainian."

Lyuda didn't say anything, just gazed at the baby girl.

Hannah put on her ring. She turned the ring so the diamond squeezed into the skin of her palm. She loved to wear her ring this way. You held onto love. You did not let go.

Lyuda cradled the baby girl. She whispered something Russian in the baby's ear. Ukrainian.

A woman across the cafe caught Hannah's eye. It was Monica from the gym. Monica threaded the empty tables. She had the same look as Hannah: tracksuit and frosted bob. She carried a to-go cup. Her other hand gripped a loop of keys and a mace sprayer.

Monica said, "Hannah! You should have gotten a homely nanny, that's what I did."

"Good grief, Monica, this isn't my nanny."

"Well, she's a lovely girl." Monica looked at Lyuda, then she leaned down to the baby in Lyuda's arms. She said, "Hi sweetie." She tried a goofy face to make the baby smile. The baby did not smile.

Monica said, "She looks so much like Keith."

Hannah held her heavy, warm mug.

"Is he like, the happiest dad?"

"Yeah, he's completely happy."

"You guys weren't hurt too bad by the downturn?"

"No."

"I had to let my nanny go. Speaking of which, Hannah, I have to get back." Monica turned to Lyuda. "Very nice to meet you."

"You did not meet me," Lyuda said.

Hannah smirked. She almost laughed. She liked Lyuda so much. She hid her smirk behind her coffee mug.

Monica paused, raised her hand to her temple. Her keys jingled. "Hold on, as I recall, you are supposed to get a pretty one, not a homely one. Yes, get the prettiest one you can find, then you have the talk with your husband so there's no question about anything. Bye, Hannah. Say hi to Keith for me."

"Goodbye."

Lyuda kissed Hannah's baby and blew on her hair.

Wow, Hannah thought, this girl was a pro. At story time, Lyuda had sat in the circle with the moms, and she had cradled her baby boy, gazing at him so long that she missed the story. She did not sing the songs, either. Maybe Lyuda didn't know American songs. Lyuda had gazed at her baby, then gazed far away, then closed her eyes. Where had her blue eyes gone?

"Lyuda, do you regret things?"

"Regret?"

"It means you feel bad about something you did. Or didn't do." Hannah reached over and took back her baby girl, who had fallen asleep in Lyuda's arms. "As for myself, I don't regret anything." She was glad to feel her baby again, soft and warm.

"Then I don't regret anything either."

"I suppose you're too young. You haven't done anything to regret."

Lyuda looked at Hannah for a long minute. "Last year, when a family let me go, I was sad. I miss those kids. But I don't regret. Happiness means more now, after being sad."

"One doesn't need to be sad to be happy." Hannah rocked her baby girl.

"But you feel differently about it."

"Is that like a Russian thing?"

"What?"

"Never mind. Did you know I was a nanny once?"

"Of course not. How would I know this?"

"That was a long time ago. After college."

"Not so long, then. And you regret it, as you say." Lyuda lifted her mug, noticed that it was empty, and set it down.

"I did not say that." Hannah was sorry she had brought it up. She said, "I'm glad it's in my past, but I don't regret it. I was—"

"You were one of the pretty ones!"

"What do you mean?"

"Nothing."

"I loved being a nanny, and I cried too when I had to quit, but I don't assign any weight to it. And I'm happy." Hannah took a breath.

Lyuda said, "You should put weight to it. No weight to your life: that is a real danger for you. Your heart needs to break to know what love is."

"Your heart has been broken? You're just a girl."

"How old am I, Hannah?"

"Lyuda…"

"Listen, we don't know each other. You did not even tell me your name. I figured it out from that Monica woman. Hannah, how much weight do you put to anything?" Lyuda lifted her mug again, but it was the same empty as before, and she set it down with a clunk.

Hannah said, "Okay, what about this. Keith regrets a few things. I can tell. He wishes he'd dated more cute girls in high school. And maybe I do too, so he would know for sure that he loved me."

Lyuda took a breath to speak, but Hannah cut her off. "But he does know he loves me. He does love me. I just wish he had played around more when he was single, so he would love me more. Regret me less."

"He regrets you, Hannah?"

"No! That's not what I meant at all."

"He's not nice to you, and he regrets you, and you don't make love."

"No, no. No. I just want him to want me more. If he'd just fooled around more, you know, before he'd picked me. I don't even know if he wonders about it." Hannah felt miserable.

"I think every boy—every man—wishes he dated cute girls." Lyuda smiled. "Do you think that Keith would ever, you know, fool around?"

"You don't ask that, missy. Keith is a hard worker, and he missed out on a lot. He could have had more. Keith doesn't want our daughter to grow up regretting anything. How does one do that?"

"You love her. You just love her."

"I do love her."

"That's very sweet."

Hannah felt Lyuda's blue eyes studying her.

"Hannah, I have to say something. You are so not right."

"Jesus, Lyuda."

"But you are so blessed, what does it matter that you are not right? You're rich. You're pretty. You have wedding ring and fine makeup. All story-time moms are pretty, I think."

Hannah said nothing. She wanted to change the subject. She said, "How much do you make, Lyuda?"

"It's Lyudka. It means something much closer. We are girlfriends now."

"Okay, Lyudka. How much?"

"Well, I don't make anything."

"You make something."

"I could tell you any number, and would you know? The truth really is I don't make anything. The parents are friends of my family, so this is what I do. Sometimes they put out money 'for lunch' or 'to go to store for eggs.' A lot of money, and I keep the change, but that's all I get."

"Do you go to college, Lyuda? Lyudka."

"No."

"And you've done this how long?"

"Two years."

"How old are you?"

"Nineteen."

Lyudka's baby was beginning to stir. Lyudka reached into the stroller compartment and got a bottle ready.

Hannah tried to ask the next question as easily. "And you don't regret any of this?"

"Wait, now you answer me. How old are you, Hannah?"

"Guess."

Lyudka giggled. "That's not polite." She lifted her baby and cradled him and said something to him in Ukrainian. The baby nuzzled and rooted at her sweater. She said the words again. She stuck the bottle in his face. He squirmed. Lyudka poked the bottle in his mouth until he took it.

"Come on. Guess. How old am I?"

"No, no. You are pretty, so it does not matter your age. All the moms are pretty. I always think so. Are you unhappy? Why are you asking me?"

"It is only a question. I don't need to be unhappy to ask you to guess my age."

Lyudka fed the baby, and Hannah told happy stories about her family. Her baby. Her husband. What was he doing right now? She invented details from the bits and pieces she knew. His walk to the bus. His workout at the gym on the first floor of the office. His work was a mystery. There were young women at work, but Hannah did not worry about them. The story she told to Lyudka was how much he loved her and how strong and handsome and kind he was, how he was thinking of her, and she knew he was thinking of her because he would telephone her at noon, and she knew what he was wearing when he called because she had picked out his suit, and she liked how his skin smelled beneath his clothes when he came home because that smell was on her skin too, and what he smelled like, above all, was her.

Keith was sweet to her. He was sweet to their baby girl. Junior partner at the firm, he made all of this happiness possible. They didn't regret anything. How many people could say that? Hannah told stories, and her baby girl slept in her arms, and the baby boy in Lyudka's arms seemed to love the sound of Hannah's voice. The baby drank his bottle and gazed, then drifted into sleep without a frown. Lyudka put away the bottle and burped him on her shoulder.

The robber came in quietly, not bursting in as they did in the movies. But Hannah knew what he was up to. From his twitchy body, she knew right away. Lyudka caught Hannah's eyes, and she turned to look, and she seemed to know it too. The man brushed past Hannah and Lyudka and cut the line at the register. He waved a gun at the barista and took cash across the counter and put it in a grocery bag. The barista brought her hands to her face and cried silently. Then the robber pointed the gun at the customers and started taking wallets. Hannah did not expect this. You never saw this in the movies. The robber moved fast, and people were backing away, holding out their wallets and purses. The last customers were Hannah and Lyudka. They stood, their babies tight to their chests, their bodies turned protectively away from the gun. The robber pointed the gun at Lyudka. She tossed her cellphone in the bag. She yanked off her silver pendant and tossed it in too. The robber pointed the gun at Hannah. She shifted her baby to one arm and tossed her wallet in the bag.

The robber said, "The ring too."

"No, please."

"Give me the fucking ring."

"Please—"

"Give it now." The man stepped closer, much closer, and Hannah felt the gun twitching, pressing hard through her frosted hair. She was crying. She shifted her baby to her hip, cradling the baby with her arm, freeing up her hands. She twisted her ring and tried to pull it off. Her hand was shaking too hard. She pulled and pulled, trying as hard as she'd ever tried anything.

"Harder, bitch!"

"It always comes right off. I don't—I mean, I can't—"

Hannah pulled until her skin bled, but the diamond ring would not come off.

"Fuck you, bitch!" the robber said and ran for the door.

He was nearing the door when Lyudka, one arm still holding the baby, grabbed her coffee mug and hurled it at the man. She nailed him on the skull, and the impact made a solid thud before the mug bounced, unbroken, on the floor. The man staggered. Lyudka picked up Hannah's mug and threw it, coffee fanning out, and she hit him again, this time in the temple, another thud. The man fell. Lyudka yelled harshly in Ukrainian, a stream of spitty words. Maybe she was cussing. Her eyes darted for something else to throw. The man got up and lurched out the door. He stumbled, dropped his bag on the sidewalk, and scrambled up. He ran away in a crooked line.

A customer ran out and collected the bag. He handed back people's things. He handed the money to the barista, which she put back in the till.

Hannah held her baby. Her ring finger ached. She had done nothing. She could never have been so strong.

Lyudka hurried over to wipe up the spilled coffee by the door. The heavy mugs were unbroken, and she picked them up and gave them to the barista, who was weeping. She used paper napkins to wipe up the mess. She held her baby with one hand and napkins in the other, and her hair fell loose from her bun. "I am so sorry. That was so—I am so sorry. I'm really not violent person. Usually this is not how I am."

The barista gave her a bottle of water. The police came and asked questions.

Hannah sat with her baby rustling in her lap. Her finger was raw, and the knuckle was swollen thick as a walnut. Her baby girl began to cry. Hannah wished she had been like Lyudka, forceful and sure, a protectress, but that wasn't what most upset her. She would go back to being happy again: that was the worst part. Hannah would go home and cry, and Keith would hold her. She was his princess. He would ice her finger until the ring slid off and on easily. Hannah would kiss Keith, lead him from the dinner table to the bedroom to mark her perfume on his skin again. But perfume would wash away.

Lyudka strapped her baby into the stroller. The baby was still asleep. Lyudka finger-combed her long hair and twisted it into a fresh, tight bun. She leaned close to Hannah. "Listen, I am nineteen, almost twenty, and I am not married. You do not understand what it means for Ukrainian girl. So, yes, I do regret things." She unlocked the brake on her stroller.

"Oh no, you don't regret anything."

"Yes, I regret! You can't understand."

"You're right. I'm blessed. But you, you're just tragic."

"What do you mean, tragic?"

"Well, I don't throw things. I wish to hell I did, but I don't. What did you yell at that man anyway?"

Hannah thought about her husband. He would come home tonight and hold her.

Lyudka said, "I regret something. You will never understand." She did not look at Hannah but found a spot on the floor and stared. "This baby, my sweet angel, one afternoon, he is crying. He is wailing. His mom did not leave breastmilk in the freezer, so what can I do? Well, I do something. I lift up my sweater, and I let him… you know. And it feels right, and he is sleeping finally, my baby is sleeping, so I do this a few more days. Then my milk comes. Now, on Sundays, when I do not work for this family, I have wet spots in my blouse in church." She began to cry. "But I will get over it. Because of this sadness, love will mean more, someday. I will find my sweet, strong man, and it will mean so much more. Next time, I throw three mugs."

Lyudka took Hannah's hand. The ring finger was swollen. "Hannah, you are the one who doesn't regret. Not really. Now who is more tragic?"

Hannah and Lyudka left the cafe. They pushed their strollers past the sewer repair, and it was necessary to go single file past the barricade. The men paused. They were the type of men who gazed at a pretty nineteen-year-old girl with full breasts and shiny blonde hair and wide blue eyes. That was easy. Everyone gazed at a girl like that. But a woman like Hannah, she got a different look, and they looked at Hannah in a tense way that was long and serious. This time Hannah looked back, because she was pretty, and pretty was her ticket, and her husband's name was on her tongue, and he loved her, and her diamond was lodged in her palm.

Lyudka turned at the corner, pushing her stroller with brisk purpose. She stopped at the bus stop that would take her to another part of town. She had taken her cellphone out, and her voice was sweet, then harsh, then sweet again. In Russian. Ukrainian. She did not look back to say goodbye.

Buena Vista (Part I)

"So go to your damn party," Jill said.

Sam gazed at Jill across the bed. Her words weren't exactly a free pass, but Sam would take them. Jill was straightening the bedsheets, tight and angry. They would fuck on those sheets when Sam got home.

Jill said, "Just go. I never know anyone at your work parties. All those slick suits. All those pretty dresses."

"They have names, you know."

"Ah-ha."

"Jill—" He wanted to see her in one of those pretty dresses. But he couldn't say it that way.

Jill had drifted over to the mirror. She zipped up her pale blue tracksuit, then zipped it down far enough to expose her white camisole. She checked her face in the mirror, especially around the eyes. She said, "In case you forgot, we have to tidy up for book club tomorrow. But if you want to go to your party, fine. If you really want to go." She gathered her hair in a ponytail. "If you'd rather."

Sam spoke to her back. "You don't even read the books. Neither do I. Nobody does." Sam bent down, retrieving this month's book where it had slid off the nightstand. He hefted its weight miserably. He said, "Last month, Monica Paré made a pass at me."

"You lucky dog."

Sam said, "Come on Jill. The party will be fun. A little break. A chance to dress up. Cocktails."

"It's all a bunch of pretend." She let down her hair and started her ponytail again.

"So let's pretend."

"Pretend what?"

"Well, for starters, let's pretend we're happy."

He wished he hadn't said that. Let's pretend something. Shadows and light. Music. Sweet taste on his tongue. His palms pressed against her hips. Her dress. Her perfume. Damn.

Jill paused, her hair in her hands, an elastic tie in her mouth. She found Sam's eyes in the mirror. "We are happy."

"Sure we are."

Jill turned around to face him. "I'm not stopping you." She shoved past him and went downstairs. She made a clatter in the kitchen.

What was he supposed to do? He knew what he was supposed to do. He was supposed to want. Want Jill. Want all of this.

Sam looked helplessly at his reflection in the mirror. How did you want what you already had?

Repair Job

Michael turned the VW microbus into the picnic grounds along Dayton Creek. He parked in the shade of the cottonwoods, killed the engine, and got out. He took it all in, the heat on his skin, the scent of cottonwood and creek water, the silence in the still air. During the past year, his memories of Wyoming had withered to such fragments, until even fragments were gone, and Wyoming had become just a word. Now it was real again. Breaking the silence, a magpie high in the cottonwoods picked its way along a branch, a dead branch, a dry, dead rattling branch. That single stray sound became part of it too. Wyoming. Michael put it all together again.

Michael knew the climb into the Bighorns would be an eight percent grade, ten percent down the back side. The old microbus had not been sounding so good in the heat. Michael walked around back, lifted the hatch, and dug his toolbox out. Karina was sleeping in the front passenger seat, so Michael was quiet. He left her there.

Chris was sprawled on the back seat. He was asleep too. "You bum," Michael whispered. Chris pulled a Mexican blanket over his head, knocking over a book with his elbow. Karina stirred. Michael left the hatch up, and he set his tools on the grass.

The Land Cruiser, with Jenny, Brian, and Artie, pulled into the picnic grounds. They got out. Brian and Artie were laughing about something. Jenny stared at Michael's tools, then at Michael, as if to say, "Really?" She suggested a walk to the ice cream parlor they had passed on Main Street. They would all go. Jenny said, "Where's Chris?"

Michael said, "He's asleep. Don't worry about him."

Karina woke up and got out. Still sleepy, she shuffled around back and snuggled against Michael. They had been dating for four months, and Michael liked her fine. Karina finger-combed her hair and gazed at the trees. Michael kissed her hair. He thought about how to fix the bus. Karina pointed at the magpie. "Michael, what's that bird?"

They walked to the ice cream parlor on Main Street in Dayton, Wyoming, and they bought double-scoop cones and ate them on the way back to the park. Karina unfolded a blanket beneath the cottonwoods, and everyone relaxed on the blanket while Michael worked on the engine. The blanket was a good idea.

Chris finally awoke, and he staggered out of the bus. He wandered toward the creek, the tallest cottonwoods with broken limbs in their crowns. Red-winged blackbirds sang along the creek. Michael had not noticed them before. He was rusty. Missed a piece.

A red pickup with an extended cab, dual axle, and horse trailer rumbled in. The trailer was decorated with streamers: red, white, and blue. Seemed to be a family heading home from a fair. Two teenage girls got out of the extended cab and walked back to the trailer. They each had long blonde hair and fluffed up bangs, and they wore red cowgirl blouses, tight Wrangler jeans, and tooled leather boots. The taller girl climbed onto the fender, reached into the trailer, and touched the horses.

Jenny looked down and spread her hands around her hips. She wore a peasant skirt and a tie-dyed T-shirt. She said,

"Could I fit into those jeans?" She tried fluffing up her hair but frowned. "I don't even know how to make my bangs do that."

Karina said, "I think those girls are cute, in a Farrah kind of way." She kicked her sneaker at a dandelion at the edge of the blanket, sent the seeds flying.

Michael crawled beneath the van. He began unbolting the engine block. Chris was no help. Michael was used to that. September of junior year, when Chris had first shown up with the bus, it was already in tow. Michael had gotten it running. Michael could fix anything. His hands were strong. They had taken the bus to Wyoming lots of times.

Michael paused his work and looked across the lot at the Wyoming girls. The younger girl had climbed back into the truck cab, but the older one stayed back with the horses. She nuzzled her face to the nearest horse's nose. She was singing to the horses. Her blonde hair glimmered in the sun. Michael's dad owned a share of a hunting lodge on the Wind River, and Michael had seen a lot of ranch girls, and they were always sweet and pretty. This girl was pretty. He liked how she conducted herself around the horses.

"How old do you think she is?" Artie was kneeling on the blanket, Michael's toolbox by his side. He held a spanner upside down.

"She's college." Brian was kneeling next to Artie. He wore tie-dye, but his hair was cut like a businessman's.

"Nah, she's high school," Artie said. "No one dresses like that in college."

"They do in frickin' Montana," Brian said.

"This is Wyoming, Mr. Master of the Universe," Artie said.

"Wyoming, Montana, same difference. Just ask Michael."

"He can't see her. He's working his magic under the hood."

"I can see her fine," Michael said. "And there's a huge difference."

"I'd like to work my magic on her," said Brian.

"Hey, don't say that!" Karina socked Brian. She scooted off the blanket and kneeled next to Michael.

"Hey yourself." Brian rubbed his shoulder.

"Karina, you're new to the gang, so let me explain," said Artie. "You have to sleep with Brian before you can sock him."

"Just ask Jenny," said Brian.

Jenny socked Brian. She laughed.

"Come on, Artie," said Brian, "you can sock me too. You know you want to." Brian blew Artie a kiss.

"Stop it, all of you." Karina looked away.

Michael thought, *Maybe this was a mistake.*

He watched the Wyoming girl run forward to the cab and climb in. As the truck and trailer drove off, Michael saw her silhouette through the rear window, then a flash of sunlight off her hair as the truck turned onto the road and drove away.

Michael slid out from beneath the VW and asked Brian and Artie to help him pull the engine. He explained that pulling an engine from a VW was routine. They agreed to help. It took all of their effort, and the engine scraped loudly and looked small and alone on the ground. Karina stepped back from the work.

Michael gazed at the engine, but he was thinking about the ranch girl.

Artie said, "Uh, Michael, you going to put that thing back together in the near future? How about before Monday? Some of us have real jobs now."

Brian looked at Artie. "Since when is saving the gay whales a real job?"

"It's a Sierra Club internship, and it is a big deal, you sell-out." Artie sat down and folded his arms.

Michael was under the bus, but only for a few minutes. He came back out.

"We can put it back in now."

"What?"

"I just wanted to get to the clutch cylinder. We're going to fry it on the hill. The extra grease might help."

They lifted the engine and bucked it back in. Michael bolted everything down. He worked in a bike shop, and he had English spanners and Italian spanners and twelve-pointed sockets, so you could do square bolts if you had to. Things fit together for him. He could make anything fit together, and as he lay on his back and bolted the engine into the compartment, he laughed, knowing he was good. Who needed a fucking real job?

"VWs are a bitch," said Artie. He held another spanner. Not the right one.

"Fucking primadonnas," said Brian. He had slid behind Jenny on the blanket, and he was massaging her neck. Jenny leaned against him.

"Fuck yes," said Artie.

"Will you guys please not talk like that," Karina said.

"Yeah, come on, guys," said Michael. Not quite done.

"Jeez, Michael, since when did you become no fun?" said Brian.

"That's the ticket," said Jenny. She leaned back against Brian and closed her eyes.

Karina nudged closer to Michael as he worked under the bus. Her hand found his leg, and Michael could tell she was tracing his tattoo. Sophomore year, he and Chris had gotten tattoos while passing through Jackson Hole. Chris had wanted to copy a passage from *On the Road* onto their backs, but they had settled for simple Indian designs on their calves. Medicine wheels. There was a medicine wheel in the Bighorns, and they would pass it in a few hours. Karina's finger went around and around on Michael's skin. A wheel.

"Guess what I heard," Jenny said. She was lolling her neck and soaking up Brian's massage. "I hear Amy Sheffield is up in the Bighorns."

"Amy?" Michael said. Almost done.

"You know. Tall Amy. Long-brown-hair Amy. Jean jacket and the French braid."

"I knew Amy," Michael said.

"She was a looker," Brian said.

Karina had stopped tracing Michael's tattoo.

"She hugged that senator who spoke at graduation," said Artie. "That right-winger dude? Alan Simpson. Shit, everybody knows everybody out here."

"Chris hugged him too, you know," Brian said. "Chris didn't know him, but he hugged him."

Jenny said, "Chris only did it to provoke him." She tossed a pebble at Michael's leg. "I hear you and Amy were a thing senior year. I hear you had something."

Brian said, "Giddyap."

"Fuck you," said Michael.

"Come on, Michael, she was a horse girl."

"Please."

Karina's hand was tight around Michael's calf.

"It was nothing," he said.

But it *was* something. Michael liked thinking about Amy Sheffield. He liked having something like that. He liked working on the engine and thinking about having that.

"A lot of guys liked her," said Artie. "I liked her."

"But you didn't score her," said Brian.

Jenny said, "Chris liked her too. Didn't they have something one year?"

"Where is Chris, anyway?" Artie asked.

"He's off somewhere, being Chris," said Brian.

"Maybe he's just sitting, you know, by the water," said Karina.

"Karina darling, Chris is never just anything," said Jenny. She pulled away from Brian and sat behind Karina. She began braiding Karina's hair. Karina held erect and still.

Michael reconnected the fuel line, and he unscrewed the cooling panels so plenty of air was getting back. There wasn't much else. He stood up. The bus would make it! It was a classic model with chrome trim, split windshield, and narrow skylights along the roofline. He thought about Amy Sheffield. They did have something. One July, he and Amy and Chris had taken the VW up into the Bighorns, and all day they had hiked up a hill, higher than the clouds, and they sat in the dry grass and watched the setting sun. Chris wandered off, the way he always did. Michael and Amy, arm in arm: that was as happy as he'd ever been.

He looked toward the gray cottonwoods. The magpie in the dead branches was gone, but magpies never did stick around.

Karina and Jenny transferred luggage and books from Chris's bus into the Land Cruiser. They went to use the park's restroom. Artie and Brian peed in the bushes and climbed into the Land Cruiser. Karina came out of the bathroom and walked up to Michael and held him. Her hands met at his spine. She always snuggled in Michael's arms in the morning, and Michael liked that, and whenever he was in a rush to get to the bike shop, Karina held tight, and Michael's T-shirt smelled like her shampoo all day.

"You can't come in the bus," he said, patting her freshly braided hair. "We can't afford any extra weight on the climb."

Karina looked down. She held tighter. "Who's going with you?"

"Chris and my tools."

"Let him go alone. You just said he'll be fine."

"Never mind what I said."

"Well, you guys go first, so we can see you. In case, you know…"

"Nothing is going to happen."

"How come you didn't tell me about this Amy girl?"

"There was nothing to tell. It didn't work out."

"Michael, you should have told me."

"Where is Chris?"

"I don't know. Apparently, I'm the last to know anything."

"It's alright. I'll find him."

Karina kissed Michael's cheek then climbed in the Land Cruiser with Brian and Artie. Michael heard Karina yell, "Knock it off!" as Brian and Artie laughed about something. Michael headed toward the cottonwoods, but he came across Jenny returning from the bathroom. She was fishing the Land Cruiser keys out of her peasant skirt.

"Nice wheels," said Michael. "Law school present from Daddy?"

"Ha ha. You're just jealous. Fix a lot of flats in that bike shop, do you?"

"Yes."

"Karina's dad owns the shop?"

"He owns a couple shops."

"Do I get a discount?"

"Where you're headed, you won't need a discount."

Jenny took Michael's hands and stepped close. Her voice was low. "What the fuck are you doing, Michael?"

"What? Karina?"

"Not Karina. You."

"Just follow us up the road, okay?"

Michael looked for Chris. He entered the cottonwoods. The air beneath the trees was cool and wet. The sound of the creek came up, a late-summer trickle from one stale pool to another. Michael stepped down the bank. Mergansers and a black-crowned heron bolted from one of the pools, and the air felt cold. Michael stepped back.

He found Chris sitting on a log. He was reading *On the Road*. Flipping through it, anyway. Senior year, Chris had disappeared for weeks at a time, and he always took the book with him. Michael didn't know how Chris had managed to graduate, but he must have pulled it together; he really did hug Senator Alan Simpson on the podium in June.

"Hey Chris."

"I don't like this book anymore."

"We got to go."

"I used to like it, but not anymore. It used to feel true, but now it doesn't."

"It's not your story. And it never was."

"How was the fix?"

"Easy. I greased the clutch cylinder. Took off the cooling panels."

"That won't work."

"It worked last time. Remember last time? Remember?"

"We'll be all right on the climb. The downhill is the real bitch." He closed the book. "So. You and Karina. There's a story. Does she ever ask about the tattoo?"

"No."

"No one asks me either. They ask about these." He held out his wrists.

"Come on, Chris. We got to go." The cold air from the creek was rising.

"You're not my keeper. Get a fucking real job."

"Come on."

One hour later, they were climbing the switchbacks into the Bighorns. Michael drove. Maybe they would make the Wind River lodge by midnight. The road was steep, and the engine was hot, whirring loudly, full throttle, but they only made ten miles per hour. It was getting dark. Jenny's Land Cruiser passed them easily, even though it was supposed to stay behind. Brian and Artie flipped them off from the passenger windows. Michael didn't see Karina. Maybe she was asleep in her blanket.

The air turned cold and thin, and the starry sky floated around them. The road climbed through rocky slopes and dark patches of forest, and the land dropped off so steeply you could see stars below you on the horizon, then farm lights and freeway lights, then the town of Sheridan glowing creamy white with dust.

Michael said, "So Jenny was saying that Amy Sheffield is up here." He had to yell over the engine's whir.

"She's on an archeology dig," said Chris.

"How would you know?"

"She still writes me," Chris said. "And I write her. She asked about you."

"About me? She asked about me? When was this?"

"Like a year ago. Do you want me to tell you what she said? I guess it doesn't matter, does it?"

"Chris…"

"I mean, the point is that she's asking, right?"

The steep climb into the Bighorns was over, and the road leveled off. The top of the Bighorns was a plateau of meadows and smooth rolling hills, and the stars became so bright you could look across the meadows and see pronghorns and deer plain as day. They passed an owl perched on a milepost, and then another. The microbus built up speed. Michael took it through its gears. The engine sounded strong.

Chris said, "Karina sure is nice."

"Yeah."

"She really loves you. Do you and Karina ever, like, talk?"

Michael drove into the night. The Land Cruiser was far ahead, in and out of view on the curves.

Michael said, "So about Amy…" The curves got worse, and he felt like he was fighting the steering wheel.

Chris said, "You still like her, don't you?"

They drove farther, and the air felt cold, and Michael turned the heat on full, but still it was cold.

Chris spoke slowly. He stared straight ahead. "Listen. The thing is, Amy and I never worked out. I liked her a lot. Maybe more than you did. I don't know. To me, that's a lifetime ago. I died and came back. And I can't think about those things anymore."

In another hour, they reached the west side of the Big-horns. The plateau began to drop off, and the dark, empty basin came into view below them. Black down there. No farm lights. No roads. No towns. The air welling up smelled like desert sage. The road descended quickly, and the red taillights of the Land Cruiser began to drop as well, but very bright from braking.

"Hey," said Chris, "Let them get ahead."

"Um, okay." Michael didn't understand, but he was up for an adventure. It would be like old times. On the Road! He slowed until the red taillights were gone.

"Douse your lights."

Even without headlights, Michael could see the road fine. Plenty of starlight. Everywhere starlight. They kept driving. Neither spoke.

When they came to a gravel side road, Chris said, "Turn off here."

Michael pulled onto the side road, and the bus bumped along. It was tough going. Michael heard something crack in the undercarriage. They climbed into a canyon. It was cold. The bus bottomed out a few times, and the clutch smelled hot.

The canyon opened to a meadow. They came upon a circle of white government trailers with a spotlight rigged on a pole. Michael stopped.

The engine cooled.

Chris pointed. "Her address is a post office box down in Shell, but I happen to know this is where she lives."

"You're fucking crazy."

"No, you're crazy, because you're going to go see her." Chris reached over and took the keys.

Michael got out. It was cold. Really cold. All he had was a T-shirt and shorts. I'm crazy, he thought. This is fucking crazy.

Chris started the engine and yanked the door shut.

Michael turned quickly. "Hey, you can't ditch me here."

Chris unrolled the window. "You're the one who got out."

"But it's a ten percent grade. You can't handle that."

"I can manage. Anyway, Shell Canyon is the real bitch. That's where it's going to happen. If anything's gonna go wrong, it's gonna be in Shell Canyon. Maybe I'll take the express." He winked.

Michael watched the bus bump away. It was really cold. What about Karina? He didn't know. He looked at the trailers parked in a circle. The spotlight was bright, and Michael moved closer to it. A tall female shadow moved inside one of the trailers. The shadow peered from the window. Michael stepped into the light. He realized he did not have his English tools and his Italian tools anymore. He wondered whether it was possible to fix anything.

The Hiding Place

The man and his wife left the motel early to visit the old sights—the bridge, the secret path, the bell tower—but they cut things short and met their daughter at her apartment around noon. It was an old brick walk-up called the Rosemont, and it was the only four-story building on University Drive, but neither the man nor his wife could recall it from their college days and anyway, they did not agree on anything anymore.

Most of their daughter's belongings were boxed and waiting by the curb. A few parents were helping their kids lug boxes and furniture, but graduation had been a week ago, and most of the rooms were cleared out. The daughter's room, on the fourth floor, was a climb, and it was one of the last ones to be cleared. Her window looked over a side lot and a row of trees. The man could see the bell tower of the university chapel through the trees, although soon the trees would be too leafy for that.

Gazing down at the lot, the man spotted a purple fairy ring in the grass. This spurred a memory. He turned from the window. His daughter's room was small, a studio. The girl was standing at the bed, folding shirts and sweaters and packing them in a box. The man walked over and stood next to her and, very deliberately, set his hands on the bed's carved footboard. It was exactly right. The bed was mounted on a track, allowing it to slide into a recess in the wall, appearing like a built-in cabinet when not in use. Exactly. His daughter's books were on the shelf above the headboard, a few novels and poetry books he knew she would never read again. The man remembered the unusual bed, and he remembered the fairy rings in the grass, and he remembered being in the Rosemont before. Back when he was in school, he had spent a night in one of these rooms, on one of these beds, on a girl's yellow sheet, his arms around her. He pulled back his hands from his daughter's bed.

"I don't fucking believe it."

"Dad!"

"Sorry. I forgot something, that's all. I mean I remembered something."

"Mom can get it. She's down at the car." The girl set down a folded pink sweater he had never seen her wear. She went over to the window and started to lean out. "What was it?"

"No, no, it's nothing like that. It's not a thing. It's not an item. It's just that I remember being here before, that's all. Listen, I'll be right back."

The girl resumed packing clothes into the box. She was humming a tune the man did not recognize. "Don't be gone long," she said. "There's a lot of boxes still."

The man went down the stairs. Solid mahogany banister. Newell post. Marble steps. Back in the day, the Rosemont must have been something special. Coved ceilings, leaded glass windows, wrought iron fixtures, mahogany trim. Now the wind blew through the empty rooms and slammed the doors. The trees along the street were shedding their catkins, and the catkins blew in and snagged on the wrought iron. At the second-floor landing, the chandelier was gone.

On the last set of stairs, the man passed two older men: the apartment manager and a priest, maybe from the local parish. They were going room to room, loading bags with college sweatshirts and books and cookware, anything good the students had left. Maybe for a thrift store. The priest's shoes clicked on the marble steps.

The man's wife stopped him in the foyer. She was carrying up a bucket of sponges and cleaners. Her face looked tired. They had argued on the drive from the motel. He couldn't remember why. He never remembered why.

She said, "We have to leave it spotless to get the deposit back."

He said, "Most of these kids just leave everything. Their whole lives, left behind."

She said, "Where are you going?"

"I forgot something."

"What?"

"Um, a letter."

"A letter? You wrote a letter? Can't you just tell her? Why do you have to make it a fucking letter?"

"It's hard to explain. But hey, guess what. I think I remember this place."

"No, you don't."

"Remember Shannon O'Brien?"

"Yeah. What about her?"

"She and I fucked in here. No, we made love."

"Fuck you, honey."

"I love you too. See you upstairs."

He went outside and around the building to the side lot. He passed the dumpster filled with books, clothes, crumpled posters, cases of empty bottles, and dented lamp shades. Someone had heaved a stained mattress against the side of the dumpster.

As the man walked across the lawn, his legs parting the tall grass, everything became familiar and focused. *Watch out for the fairy rings*, Shannon O'Brien had said, taking his hand and tugging him down a crooked path through the grass.

The man came to the utility stairs in back. The door to the stairs was unlocked. He stepped around empty bottles and a water dish the students had put out for strays. The stairs were steep and creaky and dark and narrow. He climbed three flights because he remembered three. He would know the exact door by a key hidden on a nail above the trim. Shannon O'Brien had called it her secret key, and there it was! He knocked on the door, just to be sure. Nothing. Good. He turned the key, opened the door, and tiptoed into the kitchen.

What had happened to her? Where had she gone? Was it Santa Cruz? Why did she have to meet that guy? That fucker. The apartment was quiet. He slid across the linoleum where they had sat and smoked weed and waited for cherry Pop-Tarts to bake.

He glided onto the parquet floor of the main room and ducked beneath the chandelier. Boxes from a liquor store, partly filled with books, lay beneath the windows. Dresses hung from a hook on the closet door. The front door was shut, and the latch was rattling in the breeze. A guitar in an open case lay on the floor. He slid to the bedroom. He could see the bed rolled out from the wall. He could see the ornate footboard. Exactly the same. He stopped.

A boy and girl lay asleep in the sunshine. Sheet pulled up. The girl's black hair was tangled down her cheek. The sheet was draped over their bodies, and their bodies were knotted together. The man inched forward. He put his hand on the footboard and gripped it, the patterns carved into the wood. He knew the patterns. He watched the sheet rise and fall.

He let go of the footboard and tiptoed out of the room.

Halfway down the back stairs, he met the manager coming up, and he paused on the narrow landing to let the manager pass.

"You're Alice's father, yes?" The manager was carrying a bag and stuffing it with empty beer bottles. "A nice girl, she is. None of this junk. None of those boys, tom-catting around. A nice good Catholic girl."

"She does have a boyfriend. In fact, she—"

"These are the wrong stairs, by the way. She's on the other side"

"I know."

"In that case, what are you doing up here?"

"My wife and I went to the U in the eighties. I was just—"

The manager peered at him in the dark stairwell. "Did you live here once? I don't recognize you, and I've been here twenty-five years."

"Oh, I've been here before. Say, what's that thing I saw you carrying earlier?" He wanted to change the subject.

"I found a chandelier out in the grass. It's a shame. Who would do such a thing?"

"Well, I'll see you." The man continued down the narrow stairs.

"Wait. What did you say you were you doing up here?"

"I forgot something, that's all." His hands felt empty, and he gripped the steep banister, not for balance but to have something to hold.

He went around to the front of the building, climbed the marble stairs to the fourth floor, and opened the door of his daughter's room. She was still working by the bed, but now she was packing sheets and blankets. She put a pink blanket in a box. The man remembered when his wife had put that same blanket on her own dorm bed. He had slept on it many times.

"Dad, what's wrong?"

"Nothing. But hey, check this out. There's a secret hiding place."

"What?"

"Look." He kneeled at the foot of the bed, the ornate carvings beneath his fingertips, and he pried the false panel off the footboard. The fit was tight, and the varnish on the mahogany cracked loudly, but the panel popped off. The little hiding place was empty.

"Omigod, cool. How did you know about this?" She bent down next to him, her face very close to his, and she was smiling wonderfully like a little girl. Then she frowned.

He said, "All the rooms have them."

His wife came out of the kitchen. She said, "Alice, make sure you label what goes with us, what goes with you." She went back into the kitchen. She was running water into her bucket.

The man replaced the panel on the footboard. It was tight. He fit it as good as he could get it, but it wasn't perfect anymore.

"You can sell most of my stuff, Dad."

"The CDs?"

"Some of the CDs."

"The pretty dresses?"

"The dresses, Dad." She smiled.

The girl put on a hooded sweatshirt with the university colors and 05 on the back. She reached back and pulled her braid out of her collar. Her long wavy hair, which he had always liked, was tight and pulled back now, braided. Later in the day, his wife was taking her to a salon. Probably to get one of those smooth cuts that tapered at the neck, the same as every girl. Every woman.

She was packing a dust buster. That would be good to have.

"Do you need anything?" He always asked that.

"No, Dad." She was taping the box shut.

"Are you happy?" He asked that too, and she always said yes, but he asked anyway because he wanted her to be happy even though he couldn't do anything about it.

She set down the box and looked at him. "Are you happy, Daddy?"

"Sure," he said. Damn happy. He'd better be happy. After everything that might have gone wrong in twenty-five years, he was damn happy. He thought about that night, long ago in that girl's room. They were happy. Her name was in his mouth. Shannon. They were so happy they wrote it all down on a sheet of paper and hid it away in the false panel of her footboard. Was Shannon happy now? He was happy. Everybody was happy. He was forty-six years old, and he was fucking happy. He had worked this fucking hard, he'd better be fucking happy, and he'd paid a hundred thousand to this fucking Catholic university just so his daughter could decide to... be happy. It wasn't what he'd expected, but it should have been, and he couldn't get over that. To take away all of her pain was supposed to be his job. That mattered more than being happy. It wasn't supposed to be that way, but that's the way it was. Let me take your pain.

"I don't have any pain, Daddy."

"I didn't say anything."

"Yes, you did."

His arm was around her shoulder, pulling her close the way he did when she was little, and she would cry and turn her face so he couldn't see. But she wasn't crying today. He was the one who wanted to cry.

The wife came back from the kitchen. "Did you ever find your damn letter?"

"Letter?" The girl had squirmed out of his arms, and she was placing a framed picture of her boyfriend in a small box with other pictures and letters, which she lifted carefully to her chest. She was looking at her mom and dad. She looked scared.

"I couldn't find it." He looked at the footboard.

"Well, here's some paper then." His wife held out a pad of blank paper, ready for new words.

Buena Vista (Part II)

It took forever to find the place. All these developments looked the same. The streets wound beneath lamps bright as day, and the fresh pavement was sticky beneath the car's tires. No street signs had been installed, not yet. No house numbers. No families. The houses waited, bored and empty, sparkling from spotlights at the corners of lawns too green for Colorado. Who the hell bought these pretty places? Were they happy people? Sam was lost.

He took a guess and stopped at the lone house with cars along the curb. Inside, he found the guys from sales, trolling the snack platters and talking about—what else?—sales. From the patio came the click of heels on tile: wives hiding out, cigarettes cupped in their fingers so you couldn't see the glow. A pitcher of sangria on the bar was nearly drained, and Sam had to tip it on end to get anything. Where was the hostess anyway? He knew where she was. Cramming for the goddamned book club? Sure.

After downing one drink, Sam left the party. Jill was sure to gloat about this. She probably had cleaned the whole house while he was gone. Sam would lie next to her in bed, prop up his pillow, read a little from this month's book, cross his arms, and expel a sour sigh. He and Jill would fuck on those fresh sheets and change them again before the party.

Sam was walking down the front steps when he spotted Sparrow Petrosyan coming up the pink sandstone walkway. She smiled at Sam as he passed. Sam smiled too. They stopped. Sparrow wore a little black dress. She was putting her keys in a little black purse.

Sam said, "Sparrow, you're here."

"And you're—"

He said, "You look lovely."

Sparrow said with a sunny voice, "My way to get even." She reached to touch her hair. A chignon.

"I'd say you're more than even." Sam smelled that old perfume, the one you could taste when your lips skimmed her skin, when Sparrow cried, and her tears were warm and wet on her cheek, and you kissed her there.

"Well, Sam. Too bad you're leaving." Sparrow had the prettiest voice. She stepped closer. Her heels scraped lightly against the sandstone path. The fabric of her dress crinkled.

Sam remembered how unhappy they had been. He said, "I guess I could stay a little longer."

"Sure."

"I mean, I never see you." They had been miserable.

"I know. The new project keeps me on the road." She was sweet and beautiful, and they had been a disaster together.

"Come on. I'll show you what they have. Sangria." Sam put his arm on her back and guided her in. He said, "So, did you find the place all right?"

"Fuck no!"

"Those developers. I swear, they must—"

"Shut up, Sam. Don't chit-chat me."

"I should warn you, it's all sales."

"God, I hate sales."

"Stick with me."

Noise

The intercom beeped, and the blue light flashed. Yolanda, sprawled in her hospital bed, raised her voice above the beeping and the blue. "Doc, what's it all about?"

"It's a code blue, and it's not for you." The doctor had been holding Yolanda's wrist to find her pulse, but he dropped it now. "I have to go." He parted the screen and rushed from the room. His hand left its warmth on Yolanda's skin. The screen around her bed flashed with blue, and it swished in the breeze where the doctor had gone through.

But the doctor hadn't needed to find her pulse. The frantic clicking in Yolanda's chest told all. The new plastic heart valve clicked noisily. Open and shut. Open and shut. Click click. Yolanda's heart thumped. The monitors attached to her body added their voices. She couldn't get away from the noise that said she was alive.

The priest did not leave. He remained seated in the metal chair. He was a large man, and the chair was too small for his girth. He shifted in the chair, gazed at the swishing cotton screen, and said, "Code blue means all hands on deck. The boy from the apartments isn't doing well."

"Apparently not," Yolanda said. She tried to peek through the gap in the screen. She listened to her heart valve clicking back and forth. She tried to breathe deeply to calm her heart, but her chest hurt too bad from where they had split her open. She made shallow, frightened breaths. The alarm was not for her, not this time.

The priest said, "I would go too, but I would only get in the way."

Yolanda looked the priest over. "You certainly would!"

The priest shifted in his chair. "They say he shot himself with his father's gun." He shifted again. His hand reached for his chin. "Um, I wasn't supposed to share that."

Yolanda said, "So let me tell you about code blue. I had an aortic tear, okay? Blood drained out like a garden hose. Princess Diana had the same..." She lay back. Too much talk for shallow breaths.

The priest said, "You're going to be all right."

"Not everyone crashes their car right in front of a hospital. I shouldn't be alive." Yolanda fought for the extra words, and they hurt badly, but she had to say them.

"A blessing, surely. Meant to be."

The beeping alarm would not subside. The blue light from the hallway continued to flash on the cotton screen. Light and noise seemed to barge their way into the room. The clicking in Yolanda's chest would not slow down. Some blessing! Yolanda wasn't religious anymore, but she needed to confess to someone, confess to anyone, that she was afraid. Her pain was off the charts, and she pressed the hand-held button to activate her morphine drip.

The priest pushed himself from the chair. He said, "I guess I should go down there, although I'm the last guy they want to see. It's like the grim reaper showing up."

Yolanda said, "Hey, don't go. Who pays the bills around here, the wealthy old lady with the artificial heart valve or the dumb kid from the Section Eight apartments? Ooh, made you pause, didn't I." Too much talking.

"No, you didn't." But the priest really had paused. His hand hovered at the screen.

Yolanda words came as a gasp. "He was in despair, wasn't he."

The priest switched to a soft voice Yolanda could barely hear. "Let's each worry about ourselves."

"But your whole job is to worry about other people. To crack me open!"

"My job is to give comfort."

"Father, your job is to take my fear. Oh, never mind." Yolanda waved him away. The IV in her arm swung. The morphine drip swung. The pulse oximeter swung. "Go."

The beeping alarm went silent. The flashing blue lights went dark.

Yolanda clicked her tongue in time to her plastic valve. It gave her something to think about besides the pain. Her tongue went, "Click, click, click…"

The priest was still there. He said, "You're being rather cynical."

"Well, cynical is my thing. I'm supposed to be dead. I can say whatever I want." The clicking slowed. Yolanda let her thoughts settle into a morphine haze. "We're all going to die someday."

The priest did not leave. Yolanda hurt badly, swimming in pain, but she was aware of the priest letting the screen fall, the darkness beyond, the light within, and his large body settling into the tight metal chair. "I suppose it's true," he said. He stayed.

YOLANDA SMELLED THE FOOD before she saw it. The screen opened, and the priest came in with a meal on a thick paper plate. It was a pulled pork sandwich, piled high with meat and coleslaw and smoky barbeque sauce.

Yolanda was still on Jello and crushed banana.

The priest sat down with his meal.

"Mind if I eat in front of you?"

"Do I mind if you get fatter in front of me?"

"That's not nice."

Yolanda watched the priest eat his meal. The sandwich was overstuffed and messy, and the priest worked at it slowly. Yolanda's heart valve clicked back and forth. She knew she wasn't being nice. The room smelled of barbeque and rubbing alcohol. The priest was halfway through. Yolanda was hungry.

"Can you hear that, Father?"

"No."

"Yes, you can. Come closer. Hear that?"

The priest leaned forward in his tight chair. He was so large that his dinner plate tilted on his sloping belly. The barbeque sauce began to run. "Well, I'll be! Click click!" He leaned back and caught the dripping sauce with his finger.

"Exactly. That's my new heart valve. Closer."

"That's all right."

"You smell nice, Father. Can I say that?"

"You can say that. Thank you. But it's the food that smells nice to you."

"It's tobacco, Father. I'm not dumb. I haven't used the morphine in over an hour, so I know I'm not high. You smell like fine Dominican tobacco."

The priest went back to his sandwich. He said, "So, does the clicking drive you crazy?"

"When I'm excited or nervous, it goes faster. Guess I'll never play poker again. And sex will certainly be interesting, not that I get any of that anymore. Sorry, Father."

"That's all right. I get excited sometimes too." He took another bite.

"Anyway, the clicking might be driving me crazy, but if it stopped, that would drive me even more crazy, right?"

"I hadn't thought of that."

She tried to lean up from her pillow. She whispered. "Hey, Father." Her chest throbbed with pain as she moved. She lay back. She reached for the button on the morphine drip.

"What? Why are we whispering?" The priest leaned very close.

Definitely fine tobacco. Yolanda would know the fine stuff anywhere. The priest smelled like tobacco and barbeque. Good. The smoky smells gave her mind a place to go that wasn't pain.

"Am I going to be okay?"

"I'm not a doctor. I—"

"They said this valve could last twenty years."

"That's right."

"But it could fail tomorrow."

"I don't know."

She grunted. "Can you get me a barbeque sandwich too?"

He leaned back. "Yolanda, you know I can't do that."

"How about a bite of yours?"

He looked around. They were hidden inside the screen…

THE PRIEST CAME TWICE PER DAY. And he always stayed a while. Didn't he need to visit the teenage boy from the apartments? Yolanda and the priest didn't talk much. They sat together quietly, and Yolanda's heart made its click click sound, and maybe it even went a little faster when he came around. He didn't ask questions. He ate his meals. He smelled smoky good. Maybe he didn't care about cracking her open, and maybe that was a good thing.

Yolanda tried to lean up. She said, "I want to walk around."

The priest paused between bites of blackened salmon on his paper plate. "But you're all plugged in."

She fidgeted with her IV and her morphine drip. "I can do it. I know how to do it." She lay back, eyes closed, fighting the pain in her chest.

The priest patted her clenched arm and said, "I really don't think—"

Yolanda grunted. "Looks like you could use a little exercise yourself."

"Please. No one is perfect. We are all God's children. We ought to be nice to each other."

Yolanda did not open her eyes. Her heart valve went tick tock. "No, no, no. I am not nice, and I am completely alone."

"Alone with that noise?"

"Now who's not being nice."

"Sorry. I shouldn't have said that." The priest wiped salmon from his lips.

If Yolanda didn't hurt so badly, she would have smiled.

YOLANDA OPENED HER EYES. She came back from wherever she had gone. It wasn't sleep, it was drifting in the deep blue sea, and now it was gone, but she knew from the shadows and light upon the curtain that many hours had passed. The priest was at her bedside. He was nudging her arm. The sun was bright on the other side of the curtain, and it cast rippling shapes against the fabric. The morphine drip left Yolanda confused, but it was better than the pain where they had split her ribs like yanking open a purse.

"Yolanda, it's me."

"I was swimming. Underwater, I could hear—"

"Listen, your sons are downstairs. They want to see you."

He leaned closer. Fine Dominican tobacco. His fat belly pressed the rails.

"I don't want to see them."

"But they're your—"

"Tell them to go away." The click click grew louder, faster.

"But we shouldn't want to worry them."

"Father, you don't know my family. I think they'd like to be worried."

The priest went away. The screen parted and swung closed. The sun rippled on the cotton. Yolanda heard him laughing with the nurses at the station. She stewed. She forced her mind to rise from the morphine haze. It wasn't about being rich. Yolanda would never care about her money again. Her sons could have whatever they wanted. It was simpler than that. It was this: she had been driving away from them when she lost control of the car and crashed into the side of the hospital. She had been driving in sorrow and pain, and she had floated out of her body before the impact occurred. She was never going back. Now her heart valve clicked wildly, and Yolanda fought for slow breaths. She felt herself settling into morphine again.

Yolanda's vision was dull, half-lidded, when the priest came back with a package.

"Look what they left for you!"

Her sons had left a video game console.

The priest began hooking it up to the television screen. He reached up with slow effort. He turned the screen and fussed with the cables in the back.

Yolanda mumbled, "I don't play video games."

"But your children do."

"Are you baiting me?"

"No. Just explaining."

"Do you play video games, Father?"

"Oh, yes. Everyone needs their outlet. Their diversion."

"I can suggest a healthier one for you…"

Yolanda raised her bed to forty-five degrees. She and the priest played a video game called *Grand Theft Auto*. Nice touch, kids. The priest was pretty good, or Yolanda was very bad, and he defeated Yolanda easily.

The priest said, "How about another round?"

Yolanda's car lay in a twisted, smoldering heap. Her heart valve clicked rapidly.

"Were you trying to crash?"

"Let's just say I lost control."

"Let's go another round. I want a new avatar, though."

"A skinny one?"

"That's not nice."

"I never said I was. But yes, new avatars."

"So your children—"
Yolanda clicked through avatars. "Hush."
Her clicking heart.

AT NIGHT, YOLANDA WAS ALONE, and from the click click of her artificial valve she could not escape. She could not sleep. In the hall beyond the curtain, in the light beyond the darkness, the nurses passed by. She wished the priest were still here. They could pray together for the tick tock to go away, and because two voices were twice as loud as one, they could pray for many more things. They could pray that her sons would love her and not her money, that the pain where the doctors had split her ribs would go away, and that the priest would be so happy he did not need to indulge in cigars or second helpings. No, let him have his second helpings. And Yolanda would ask to hear his story, about a life that would have been quite different if he had made other choices, because Yolanda already had her different life now, and it had come in an instant when she was beyond making choices. She had never asked for this heart valve, this click click. Yolanda would crack open the priest like the doctors had cracked her.

YOLANDA WAS WAKING. She must have fallen asleep again. Came back from the ocean again. She was lying in her bed. There was light and shadow, and there was rubbing alcohol, and the nurse was changing something at her side. A fresh bladder bag? More morphine to drip into her arm? The doctor came in and took Yolanda's pulse. The skin of Yolanda's arms and legs had turned purple and blue, blotchy like a bruise. Wounding from the crash? But the doctor said no, it was the blood thinner they were giving her for the heart valve. And it wasn't right. They needed to look into this. Yolanda wanted them out of the room. She wanted the priest to come. She wanted her skin clean and brown. She wanted tobacco and a fat pork sandwich on a hoagie roll.

YOLANDA AND THE PRIEST WATCHED a nature show on PBS. It was about whales. The blue whale. The largest animal of all time. The priest ate his hoagie roll and watched the nature show. Yolanda sipped grape-flavored Gatorade through a straw.

The priest muted the sound. "When I was little, people made fun of me for being fat. They called me a whale. I hated whales then, but now I like them." He pressed unmute, and the sound came back. Gentle music and a man with an English accent.

Yolanda's heart valve clicked calmly.

"Father, why are you here?"

"What do you mean? It is a calling."

"No really. It's the commissary, isn't it? That's your thing. You love it there. They give you extra-large servings because they like you. Then there is the coffee shop, and the magazines. There is the nice artwork in the lobby. You like hanging out at the nurse's station. All the nice people. You get to see people, and they are all very nice. Except me. But anyway, your life is like a nice vacation. I'm sure the bathrooms are amazing and clean. Vacation from what though, don't you ever wonder?"

The priest rose from his chair. He set down his plate. He came close. He said, "It sounds like you already know why I'm here."

They watched the slow glide of blue whales.

Yolanda took the remote from the priest and pressed the mute. The whales glided silently, and Yolanda told the priest a story. "When I gave birth to my first son, the medical plan said I could stay five whole days, and I sure as hell did. Sorry, Father. I could have left on day three, but hell no! I asked for the chaplain then too and got one, and he prayed and prayed for that little baby because he was not baptized. The chaplain said all the right things about that, and about everything else. And I did not want to leave. But they put the baby in my arms and that was that. And oh, he cried. And I cried too."

Blue whales breached and breathed.

The priest said, "We're finally getting somewhere."

"Don't jinx it, Father. Back to whales."

Yolanda had not pressed her morphine button in a long time.

She said, "So how's the boy from the apartments?"

"Remember, I'm not supposed to—"

Yolanda didn't wait. "When I was little, I was in the hospital. I don't even remember why. They brought me a stuffed bear, braided my hair, did every sweetness. Told me every fib a frightened child needed to hear. Like I said, I don't even remember why I was there, but it was nice. I would go back to that... in a heartbeat. It was so fine, to be cared for. Now this god-damned heart valve makes life into a joke. It's like having a Barbie doll part inside, but it's the only thing between me and the end of everything. I really don't want to leave."

"We could play another video game."

"No, just give it to the boy. All of it."

"That's very kind."

"Last kind thing I'm ever going to do."

Yolanda unmuted the nature show. She had learned a lot about whales. At one time, the whales could walk on land. They elected to go back to the sea. Come up for air now and then. They hardened into these changes. Nowadays, if the whales came back on land, if they beached themselves, it was a terrible mistake.

An orderly came for the video game, the cables, the controllers. He said nothing about the boy.

THEY TOOK YOLANDA OFF JELLO and mashed banana. It was Mexican night, and Yolanda ordered the enchiladas rojas. She ate with the priest. He set her plate on her blue bruised lap. A single, lonely enchilada. The priest knew all about Mexican night, and he had ordered the enchiladas too. His plate came with a heap of rice and beans.

"Geez that's a lot of food."

"I brought an extra flan for you."

"Thank you."

"I'm nervous," he said. "I eat when I'm nervous." The priest was already picking at Yolanda's flan.

Yolanda said, "You're feeding your wants and needs, except maybe the celibacy one." Her breath did not feel good, and the words came hard. Too much talking yesterday. They should have kept her on the Jello.

"I don't suppose you'll want to pray? Because I think you need to pray."

"Please, Father."

Her family came after the commissary closed. No wonder the priest was nervous. He had known they were coming. Yolanda put up with her children, bouncing her grandchild on her black and blue legs, and it was crowded inside the curtain, and there was too much talking to hear the valve go click click. Her sons were telling noisy stories, and the priest was chuckling along nervously and shifting his bulk in his tight chair, but the only thing Yolanda wanted to hear was her own heart going click click. So she made up her own noisy story and said the black and blue didn't hurt but that the doctors were checking it out, and everyone should leave. And then a voice added to her story and said the risk was a hemorrhage in her brain, or in her lungs, or even in her eyes. And she needed to stay relaxed. Jesus Christ, she had been relaxed. If only they could be quiet for a few seconds and everyone could please listen.

The family left, and there was silence. Click click. The priest sat in the metal chair. His hand went to his mouth. Then he patted his shirt pocket.

Yolanda said, "This must mean I'm near the end. If they send a lawyer—"

"Are you hurting?"

"Yes. Yes." Yolanda looked for words and found the breath for a tiny wail.

SHE STARED AT THE ACOUSTICAL TILE. She stared at the shapes the sun made on the cotton screen. She closed her eyes. It was morning, and she was talking with the priest, and he would have left for another patient, but Yolanda grabbed his arm, his cool skin surprising her, and she said to stay. She did not want to pray. But the priest folded his hands over Yolanda's hands and made a long prayer, loud, and now Yolanda was praying, digging her nails in, but she was praying for silence, not words, and there was her click click, speeding up, slowing down, between verses of the Bible and good words about health and family and eternal life. Her legs under the sheets were covered with blue as the bruises blossomed. Her anticoagulants had done too much. Was there a reason? There didn't need to be a reason. Was there a reason the acoustical tile was white, and you couldn't see anything beyond it, and you could hear the hum of the priest's words above the clicking from inside? For days, she had hated the click click. Now she wanted it to be the only sound. Her heart valve slid back and forth, back and forth, assured her she was alive.

The prayer ended in Jesus' name. Now the priest was the one short on breath. Now he was the one saying, "I don't like it. It's not a click click. It's a poke, poke, poke."

Yolanda said, "It's okay, Father. Just listen. That noise in my chest is my promise."

"Shall we pray some more?"

"Not a single word."

THE PRIEST CAME BACK IN THE EVENING. He sat down. The room was dark, and he pulled the cotton screen extra tight. Down the hall, coming from the boy's room, the sounds of *Grand Theft Auto* boomed and screeched.

The priest asked, "Are you afraid?"

Yolanda was dry-smoking one of his beautiful Dominican cigars. It was dark and cool and delicious. She clicked extra morphine and found the strength to breathe deeply. Smoke was silence, breath without words.

She said, "So let me tell you a story about being afraid. We were in Hawaii. Well, I was in Hawaii. This was after the divorce, so I went to Hawaii by myself. It was a charter boat, and we—I mean I—was snorkeling off the Napali coast. I was deep in the water, and when I came up, the charter boat was gone. There was only the water. Everyone was gone. The guides, the other tourists, gone. And I thought, this is how it ends. There was only the water. And you know what? It was so quiet above the water. Not even any wind. I couldn't take it, all that quiet. So what did I do? I dove. I listened under water, and I could hear my own heartbeat. That was something. I couldn't get away from it. And then I heard something else. The whales. So much noise they were making. Clicks and groans and the siren song. We heard the same things on the nature show, right? But let me tell you what lay under it, let me tell you what all that noise was obliterating. The beating of their hearts. I heard their hearts beating. And just like us, maybe they make a lot of noise because they cannot function any other way, because who wants to think about your heart beating all the time? Well, I do now, but not then, and not the whales. You want it to happen, but you don't want to think about it. Anyway, the charter boat came back, and I was saved. Everyone must have felt horrible. No one sat by me. Nobody said anything. That silence all over again. The noise of the boat's engine was a rage, and I think we welcomed it. You didn't have to feel anything at all."

The priest sucked at his dry cigar.

Yolanda said, "There is no truth in the content of words, there is only the noise provided by the telling of them."

They sucked their cigars. Yolanda's heart valve clicked smooth and slow.

"Same with your prayers, Father. Noise."

"Maybe."

"I don't need your prayers. I don't need whales. Or my family. Or my money. I don't actually have any money, Father, not anymore. All I need is this click click."

THE BOY FROM THE APARTMENTS was getting out today. He was being moved to skilled nursing. There were balloons. Nobody was keeping it confidential now. Same with Yolanda's black and blue. She had heard the nurses talking. Yolanda's screen was wide open, and the morphine made her high as a kite, but she saw the blurry boy being wheeled out. Maybe she saw the game console on his lap, and she heard them talking about him, about her.

The priest declared it a miracle.

Yolanda said, "Don't ask me what I believe."

The priest said, "Life is about easing pain. Doesn't matter what you believe."

"But you have to admit, that's a rather low bar." She pressed the button for more.

He whispered. "I brought more cigars. And there's another show about whales…"

Yolanda whispered back, "No one's wheeling me away."

IN THE MIDDLE OF THE NIGHT, Yolanda couldn't sleep. The room was dark and quiet as the deep blue sea. She wanted to go back to the sea. She wanted it right now. She listened to her heart. She looked up at the monitors attached to her body. They looked okay. She listened to the click click in her chest. It sounded okay. But she knew from the blossoming darkness in her vision that she was not okay and she would not be going to the deep blue sea. There were fat dark shapes forming in her vision, blocking out the cotton screen. She smelled iron, not the sweet Dominican tobacco. Yolanda's thoughts were interrupted by a flash of light, and she felt a blast of pressure and pain in her skull. It was the wrong last thing to feel. Then came the wrong last thing to hear, not the click click of her own brave heart, but the code blue beeping, loud and shrill and just for her.

Soft and Warm Against Me

Jimmy and I were heading out the door when the phone rang. We should have let it go, but maybe the girls needed us to bring something. We were always loaning them stuff: textbooks, records, weed. You never knew. Their apartment was on the same airshaft, and we always heard them chattering, or drawing a bath, or crying on the phone. Sometimes they even yelled up to borrow stuff, but mostly they phoned or came to the door. Sarah and Elizabeth. They both had blonde hair and blue eyes, and they were always swapping sweaters, so it was easy to mix them up. They always smiled when you handed them what they needed, and we were always glad to help them.

I picked up the phone.

"Matthew, is that you?"

My mom.

"Can't talk, Mom. We're in a hurry."

Jimmy said, "Shit!" He stomped over to the window. The snow was falling hard, choking the light from the streetlamp. Jimmy fished through his pocket and took out his pipe. He lit a bowl with his vintage lighter. Orange flame lit up his face. You could smell kerosene and brass.

"Hey, over here." I held out my hand.

My mom said, "What?"

I said nothing.

She said, "Matthew, you know what tonight is."

Jimmy came back from the window and handed the pipe to me. I took a hit, marijuana and kerosene stinging my lungs.

My mom said, "Matthew, you ever think about your sister anymore?"

Robert, my other roommate, came out of his room. He wore his leather jacket, and he smelled like cologne, the good stuff he never let us borrow. One look at Jimmy and me, and he rolled his eyes. He took Jimmy's pipe and helped himself to a hit.

"Matthew?"

I said, "Mom, I got to go."

Robert exhaled. "Little boys," he said.

"Where are you going that you can't talk to your own mother?"

"What the fuck," Jimmy said. He flipped his lighter open and shut, open and shut. The lighter made a sliding metal sound, and the orange flame of kerosene flashed in the dark.

"These girls are having a party, Mom."

A pause on the line. "My golden-haired daughter is murdered. Two years, the memory burns. My son, he amuses himself at a party."

"Mom!"

"She used to tell you stories. Remember her stories, Matthew? But how can she tell stories now when she's so alone? I mean, of course she's not alone anymore. Sweet Jesus." My mom choked up.

Jimmy glared at me and made the cut-off sign across his neck.

Robert took another hit from the bowl, the embers glowing.

"Mom, we really got to go."

"To your party. Go to your damn party."

Robert shoved his way between me and Jimmy and out the door. Kerosene, weed, leather, cologne. He never told us where he was going. He would smell like a girl's perfume when he returned in the morning.

"Your uncle's over from Philly. Matthew, I tell you—"

Jimmy waved the lighter under the phone cord. Smoke rose from the cord. The melting plastic dripped onto the floor.

"Jesus Christ!" I pulled the cord away, but the signal had cut off. I was ready to cry. My sister, I had totally forgotten. Girls. Weed. Weakness of the soul.

Jimmy patted my back. "Two things, bro. Never talk to your mom when you're stoned, never be late for a party where you could score, and never keep your roommate waiting."

"That's three things, Jimmy."

"Let's go." He clicked the lighter shut, and the room went dark.

We took the stairs two at a time. When we reached the first floor, the cold was pouring in from the street. Someone had propped open the main door by wedging a Shakespeare anthology under it. Jimmy said, "Dude, that looks like your book." And it was. The goddamned girls.

Snowflakes blew into the hall, settled on the tiles, and melted away.

Jimmy knocked on the girls' door.

I said, "I'm fucked, Jimmy."

"Dude. You only took one hit."

"No. My sister—" I felt horrible about it. Standing in the hall, shifting my feet to keep warm, stoned good, I couldn't even find the word that was my sister's name. I wanted to run out that door into the night and keep on running. The cold and wind would hurt more than anything, but that's what I deserved.

"We should have brought some beer," Jimmy said. "The girls don't have ID."

I said, "They don't need ID." I made the outline of a girl's figure with my hands. Tits and waist and hips. "Any clerk who cards Sarah is gay."

Jimmy said, "Elizabeth's the hot one."

I said, "Which one's Elizabeth?"

Jimmy said, "We are so fucked."

We laughed. I felt terrible about laughing. Then we heard music and voices in the apartment, and we let ourselves in, and I forgot about feeling terrible for a while.

The room's heat hit me in the face. Heat and cinnamon and clove. We didn't see Elizabeth and Sarah at first, just three guys hovering by the kitchen door. They wore hockey jerseys, the kind you buy at the bookstore, your graduation year printed on the back. Two 85s and an 86. The boys were talking hockey and drinking Coronas, which they gripped around the neck. You always saw empty Coronas by the dumpster. The boys were gazing into the kitchen. Something good in there.

"Shut the damn door."

An older man was sitting in the girls' papasan chair. He wore a tight tweed jacket and a tweed coat over it. He drank from a dark bottle. He glared at me.

I shut the door.

He said, "That's better." Maybe it was the dope, but I swear he kept glaring at me.

Elizabeth came in from the kitchen. She nudged between the hockey boys. She wore an apron over a plaid skirt and pink sweater, and her face was flush. We hugged. My hands slid across her long smooth hair.

Elizabeth flopped on the couch. "It's fucking hot in there." She wore a silk scarf knotted around her neck, and she tugged at it.

My hands remembered the smoothness of her hair. I was stoned good.

Sarah came in from the kitchen. She looked like Elizabeth, but she wore a blue sweater with a white turtleneck beneath, the collar mussed around her throat.

She looked straight at Jimmy.

Jimmy looked straight at her.

One of the hockey boys said, "Don't get any ideas. She's dating her professor."

Sarah turned and glared at the hockey boy. Then she gazed at Jimmy.

"And her daddy's the college president," the hockey boy said. He was skinny, and his hockey jersey hung loose around his body. He looked like a little boy.

Sarah held out her hand, and Jimmy took it. Sarah smiled. You just knew Jimmy's other hand was on that brass lighter in his pocket.

The tweed man in the papasan chair coughed. He shifted his body, and the chair groaned. Why was he still glaring at me?

The boys went back to talking hockey. There was a game tonight at the arena. Sarah and Elizabeth's place was a pit stop. Good. I didn't like those guys. Let them go. The night was young.

I said, "Cool party," but it was only something to say.

Elizabeth said, "We're baking apple pie." Her fingers twirled the end of her scarf.

I looked around the room. Me, Jimmy, Tweed Man, the hockey guys, the girls... I said, "Big enough?"

Tweed Man laughed, but I didn't mean it to be funny. I wanted some pie. He was laughing at me, and I wanted some goddamned pie.

I dropped beside Elizabeth on the couch. Sarah sat on the other side, and she gathered her skirt so Jimmy could sit, but the couch was small, and Jimmy had to squeeze in. Jimmy and Sarah were talking, their heads bent so close together you couldn't hear.

I said to Elizabeth, "Is her dad really the president?"

"Yes."

"Golly."

Elizabeth said, "Golly? Golly? Little boy, who the fuck cares? Don't you want to know whether she's dating her professor? I would rather want to know that if I were a guy."

"Okay then. Is she dating her professor?" I felt Tweed Man's eyes on me. I was still trying to remember my sister's name, and all I could think of was this tight, tweed, wheezing man.

"Never mind!" Elizabeth rolled her head against my shoulder and closed her eyes. Her hair was warm. She opened her eyes and gazed up at me. Her lashes were long and curved. She said, "Matthew, did you bring some?"

And I knew. I knew the word. I said, "Jennifer."

"Excuse me?" Elizabeth pulled away.

"My sister's name. I just remembered. I mean, you look sort of like my sister, Jennifer. You see—" How did I explain this? I was aware of my hands forming a gesture, trying to form one, anyway. I set them down.

"You're a cute boy, Matthew, but you are clueless." Elizabeth put her hand on my knee and pushed herself off the couch. She walked over to the hockey boys and took a swig from one of their beers. She propped her other hand on her hip and glanced at me over her shoulder. I didn't care. I had remembered my sister's name, goddamn it. I felt triumphant. I gazed around the room. Tweed Man really was glaring at me.

Elizabeth wandered over to the stereo. She knelt, her plaid skirt spreading around her, and she flipped through the records. Her long hair fell over one shoulder. "Matthew, suggestions?"

I didn't say anything. Half those records were mine. The room smelled sweet and warm with cinnamon and apple and butter and clove. Why was she asking me?

Jimmy got up, quick-stepped into the kitchen, and came back with three beers. He handed one to me, kept one for himself, and handed one to Sarah. I was glad to drink on their dime. I thought about the pie baking in the oven. I got hungry thinking about it.

I said, "Elizabeth and Sarah. That's so preppy."

"What did you say?" Jimmy said.

"The names. And the sweaters and kilts and the smooth hair."

"Will you shut up, stoner?" Jimmy looked at me hard.

Tweed Man chuckled. He drank from his dark bottle. His tweeds bulged around his ribs, and his chuckle gurgled out. He inhaled with a rasp.

From the kitchen came a billow of smoke. Elizabeth got up from the stereo and ran into the kitchen. The music started up. She had put Squeeze's *Singles* on the turntable.

Tweed Man gurgled again.

The skinny hockey boy blurted at Sarah. "So if you're the president's daughter, did you grow up in the mansion? Did you have servants and stuff?"

Sarah opened her mouth to speak, but a second hockey boy interrupted her. "I heard that place is haunted."

"Everyone says that..." Sarah looked away. Her fingers reached and tugged the collar of her turtleneck.

"A girl was killed in there." This hockey boy was muscular and short, and his jersey hung to his knees, another little boy.

Sarah sat back and pursed her lips.

Elizabeth came in with more beers. She kept one and gave one to me. "Wait, who was killed? What's happening?" She looked around like she was confused. Her own apartment, and she was confused.

I guzzled down my first beer and started in on the second.

"Did you ever hear stuff at night?" The muscular hockey player continued.

"No!"

Jimmy produced his pipe and lighter. It had been his dad's lighter, and his uncle's lighter before him. It was from the war, and—I don't know. It was something he could do with his hands. I wanted something. I picked at the label on the neck of my beer.

Elizabeth squirmed in next to me, folding her knees under her skirt. She leaned against my shoulder, heavy, maybe drunk. She smelled like cinnamon and butter. My heart was beating fast.

The little hockey boy stood before Sarah, too close. He said, "The mansion was built by some newspaper baron, before it became a college. His daughter was strangled by a psycho."

"How the hell would you know this?" I asked. I stiffened my shoulders. I didn't like him so close to us, me and Jimmy and our girls. Because that's what they were. They were our girls now.

"I used to give campus tours to incomings. I've been in there."

"Why don't we just ask her?" I pointed to Sarah.

Our girls.

"I'm not participating." Sarah slumped down.

Tweed Man took a swig from his bottle.

Jimmy set his pipe in Sarah's lap. She picked it up and looked closely at it, her chest rising and falling under her blue sweater. Short breaths.

The hockey boy waved his little arms as he talked. "So the girl was named Veronica, or something, and she was beautiful. There's a painting of her in the foyer."

"That much is true," muttered Sarah.

"And the girl's dad, he never let her outside. She had tutors, and she was like a bird in a cage."

Jimmy's lighter made its sliding metal sound. Sarah's breath sucked in deeply.

"So how did she die?" one of the other hockey guys asked.

Sarah exhaled. "Jesus Christ."

The hockey boy went on. "There was this dude, he broke into the mansion. He knew about a secret tunnel because he was like a stonemason who'd worked on the place. He knew about the girl. She was taking a bath when he burst in, and he dragged her into the tunnel and strangled her. There was a shootout with the cops, but the gunshots made the ceiling come down, and the girl and the man were never found. They sealed off the tunnel after that."

"So how do you know she was strangled?" I said. My hands. I really wanted something for my hands. I put an arm around Elizabeth and her smooth hair. She leaned in.

"Well, my dad is on the board. He took me through there once. There's still a secret door, and you can see stuff. And it is totally haunted."

"Your daddy's not on the board!" Elizabeth said. Her arm tensed against my shoulder. Her sweater was soft. Her pink sweater.

"And there's no secret tunnel," Sarah said.

"Is too," Hockey Boy said. "And I've seen it." He did not look at anyone as he said this, and his lips got firm and white.

"Is not!"

"Is too!"

I said, "What is this fucking 'board?' that everyone's dad is on?" Stoned out of my gourd, and I couldn't keep my mind still. I couldn't keep my mouth still.

Tweed Man was gurgling. A thread of spit dripped on his tight clothes.

"Will you shut up, old man!" one of the hockey players said.

Tweed Man clenched his bottle. He tensed in his bulging clothes. The wrinkles in his jacket tightened. I felt his tightness. I felt the gurgle in my own throat.

Elizabeth was leaning against me close and soft and warm, and she let me tighten my arm around her. She looked up.

Her face was flush. I felt strong. I clenched my beer bottle in a fist. Elizabeth took my fist and laid it across her waist. Her sweater was soft, and I could feel her breathing. Her hand was warm over mine. I opened my fist.

The record ended. The boys finished off their beers, gathered their jackets, and left for the game. They left mad. They weren't getting anything.

"Do you know those guys?" I asked. "Those punks." I felt so strong.

"Oh yeah, they loan us stuff all the time."

"Oh."

Jimmy rose. He tossed me his pipe, his vintage lighter, and his film canister of weed. He took Sarah's hand and helped her up. Sarah smoothed her hair around her shoulders. Her hair was bright and blonde against her blue sweater. She led Jimmy toward a bedroom. She stopped. She closed her eyes and frowned and said, "Wait. Not that one," and pulled him toward the other bedroom.

Tweed Man watched them go.

Elizabeth nuzzled my chest.

"So if her dad is the president, why doesn't she just live at home?" I asked.

"That's a silly question, boy." She brought her face close and pressed her lips to my ear. She said, "Matthew, let's smoke some!"

I was already stoned, and everything felt dark and warm and close, and Elizabeth was soft and warm against me. I packed a bowl for her, and she took a long hit and handed it back. I took a hit, and I tasted her wet mouth on the pipe, sweet and sticky and cinnamon. We put down the pipe and kissed, and her tongue tasted the same as her lips. I stroked her hair, and it felt warm and smooth and soft. We sat back and drank beer.

Tweed Man got up. He buttoned his tight tweed coat over his tight tweed jacket.

"So, what do you teach?" I asked him.

Elizabeth said, "Matthew, no. Oh dear boy, oh dear."

"It's a fair question. Why is he here?"

"Matthew."

Tweed Man glared at me, and my stoned brain knew he was asking me the same thing. Why was I even here? Well, I knew exactly why I was here. I knew what I was trying to forget, too, what I was trying to remember and forget at the same time. Tweed Man left. Cold air washed into the room.

A timer went off, and Elizabeth stumbled into the kitchen and came out with a huge apple pie, steaming, tilting, dripping off the side. It was the widest, deepest, gooiest apple pie I'd ever seen. Elizabeth wore pink oven-mitts, and she set the pie on the coffee table. "There's another pie after this, too."

"Who the fuck?" I pointed at the door.

"That was Old Man Bill. He lives one floor up. He's on the same airshaft as us. He's in the hallway all the time. If you stopped ogling girls once in a while, you might notice such things."

"That's what you call him? Old Man Bill? He's such a charmer."

"Did you know he has a gun? I held it once."

"What kind of gun does he have?"

"What kind of gun? Well, let's see. A black one? It was warm and rather heavy. By the way, he likes you." She smirked.

"What's so funny?"

"He likes you because he knows you're not getting anything tonight!" She giggled.

"I might get something." I tried to hold her gaze, but my hopes were fading fast. "Maybe?"

"Oh my god, Matthew!"

We each took a fork and dug into the pie.

Elizabeth said, "If you must know, I'm the one sleeping with my professor. But I cut off that arrangement. I was rather mean about it, really. Kissing boys right in front of him after class! But what the fuck could he do about it? Besides, Old Man Bill has a gun. I'm telling you, he would look out for us. I really should take him some pie."

"You've never brought us any pie." I was trying to remember if I'd ever smelled pie in the airshaft.

"You shouldn't keep track of such things, little boy."

We ate a ton of pie, right from the pan. So hot it burned. Elizabeth drank my beer, which was technically her beer, and she leaned against me, her skin warm. She had sticky apple juice on her mouth, and so did I. We smoked another bowl, and we kissed, sweet and sticky.

I said, "My sister used to make pie."

"You have a sister?"

"Well, yeah. I mean—"

Elizabeth grabbed my hand. Her mouth was full, but she looked like she wanted to say something. She swallowed the bite and stuffed in another. "I've been in that mansion a million times, and I can tell you there's no tunnel. That whole story was bullshit."

"My sister was—"

"Did you know my dad is on the board, too?"

I reached up to Elizabeth's neck and untied her scarf, sliding it away from her skin. She held still, but her body was teetering. The scarf was gauzy and pink, and it sparkled as I dangled it in the air. We watched the sparkling pink scarf for a long time. The music stopped.

I took another hit. "So my sister baked the most amazing pies. And her name was Jennifer." Elizabeth nestled against me, and she was so warm. "And she was pink and soft and warm like you." Elizabeth closed her eyes. "But then she decided she wanted out, wanted out of everything. Being alone hurt more than anything she had ever felt in her life, but lately she had begun to feel nothing at all, as if her heart were hollowed out with a spoon." Elizabeth's body softened.

I kissed her hair. My voice was a whisper. "And the princess ran from the castle, ran farther still, towards the sunshine, ran over a snowy hill, and was never seen again."

"Matthew." She put her fingers on my lips.

"I'm serious. Every word. She used to tell stories. She was—"

We kissed some more. I clenched that scarf in my fist.

"She met this motherfucker..."

Elizabeth said, "So your other roommate. Robert. The player. Now there's a motherfucker. Old Man Bill hates his guts."

She took the empty pie dish to the kitchen and brought out the next pie. She almost tripped and spilled the whole thing. It had cooled some, and she set it in her lap. The crust had rumpled around the lumpy apples inside, and it looked like the skin over a man's knuckles. She poked the crust with her finger. First came the good cinnamon smell, and then a wisp of steam. Finally, a bubbling sugary goo bled across the crust. The wisp of steam hung in the air like a ribbon, then twisted away.

We watched the pie. Elizabeth said, "So my professor said to me, 'Someday you'll be old and alone and cold.' Isn't that funny? And I'm twirling the ends of my hair, and I remember this exactly because he grabbed my hand and said, 'Don't you dare taunt me, Sarah,' and I yelled, 'Don't you tell me not to do anything.' And I go on twirling my hair. Isn't that mean of me? I don't care."

"I thought she was Sarah—" I pointed to the bedroom door.

"Oh my gosh, Matthew! No! Hold on a second." She set the pie on the coffee table and went into the bathroom. I was staring at that pie. She was in the bathroom a long time. She came back, kneeled at the stereo, and put on Squeeze again. She slumped beside me, and we kissed, but her mouth tasted like peppermint now, and I knew what she had been doing in the bathroom. She lay against my shoulder, and we watched the bouncing lights on the stereo, and I watched the second pie on the coffee table steaming, and I wanted the peppermint taste out of my mouth. I was still holding her little pink scarf.

"Matthew, I am such a mess."

"You have no idea." Everything was blurry, and I was stoned, and I forgot my sister all over again. Did she really tell stories? Was she really soft and warm? Maybe that's why I got high, so I didn't have to worry about how much I'd forgotten. I would sit by the airshaft and smoke Jimmy's weed and listen to the girls' voices floating up the shaft, and wonder which preppy girl was splashing in the tub, wearing her Walkman and singing The Pretenders out of tune, and I would rest my head against the hatch of the airshaft and gaze into the cool gray light going down, down, and I could tell when the girls were smoking, or crying, or puking their dinner into the toilet, or maybe just braiding their hair, or talking on the phone to their mom and dad on their fancy cordless telephone, begging for more money, or talking to boys, or professors, apparently. Not talking to me.

"Matthew—"

"Not everyone gets old, Elizabeth. To hell with your damn professor."

"I'm not Elizabeth." She giggled. "Oh my gosh, you are such a silly boy." She closed her eyes and rested her head on my shoulder. Her blonde hair was spilling down her back, spilling down her chest. She slid her hand down and began rubbing my cock through the fabric of my jeans, slowly, firmly, and it got hard, of course it got hard, and she worked it upward in my jeans and unbuckled my belt, but then her hand began to slow.

"I am not silly," I said.

She worked her hand up and down smoothly, then her breathing became slow and regular, and her hand slid away. Her soft warm body slumped against mine.

"She was going to NYU. She was living in the city. She met this guy, the motherfucker…"

This girl named Sarah slept. Everything was blurry, and she was golden hair and soft pink sweater, and I held her tight only to have something to hold. I decided to wait for Jimmy, and I watched that pie cooling on the coffee table. Man, I wanted that pie. The record had ended, and the needle was popping, but with the girl sleeping against me I couldn't move. I pretended she and my sister were friends, and they were talking about boys and laughing, but I had to pretend really fucking hard or it didn't seem real.

Jimmy came in from the bedroom. He scooped up his lighter and his pipe. When he saw my unbuckled belt, he smiled at me.

"You bad boy."

"You're the bad boy."

"Dang girl fell asleep. I fell asleep too. Shit, I got nothing."

"What did Shakespeare say? 'Inspireth the act but taketh away the ability?' You should haveth some pie."

"I will taketh some pie." Jimmy took a fork and ate from the dish.

There was a tapping at the door, and Robert came in. Cologne. Leather jacket. Cold air. Perfume. He stared at us and the girl and the pie.

"You fucking losers," he said. Then he pointed at the girl asleep against me. "Now's your chance, boy."

"Want some pie?" I said.

"Don't mind if I do." Robert knelt by the pie and took up a fork. "Unlike you twerps, I've earned it tonight, if I may say so myself."

With my foot I pushed the coffee table away. I pushed the pie away. I said, "You can't have any."

"What did you say?"

"You heard me. Now get the hell out of here. Get the hell out, right now."

Robert stood. He faced me. He waited.

Jimmy's lighter nervously flashed. Orange kerosene.

Elizabeth, or Sarah, or whatever her name was, she whimpered and nuzzled against me, but soft and warm was all she was, and soft and warm weren't enough anymore. None of this was enough. I slid away from the pink pretty girl, and I lay her sleeping body gently on the cushions. I stood to my full height, facing Robert, and I resolved to make a fist, and I was glad this meant releasing the sparkling scarf from my hand.

Buena Vista (Part III)

Sam gave Sparrow a heavy glass. She tipped it up, her eyes observing him over the rim.

"You look handsome, Sam."

"Gee, Sparrow."

"I can say that, can't I?"

"As long as I can say you're totally stunning."

"Well, of course you can." The corners of her eyes wrinkled with a smile.

"Anyway, you are."

Sparrow took his hand.

Sam said, "Yeah, you're stunning, and I have book club tomorrow."

"Bingo!"

He looked at his empty glass.

"Sam, are you ever going to talk to me when you're actually happy?" Sparrow's hand had not left his.

"I mean, I don't even remember the name of the book. I do remember there's bricks on the cover and—"

"So spill it, Sam. Where's Jill?"

"Where's Tony?"

Their grip became tighter.

They discussed work for five seconds. Sparrow finished her glass, and they snuck into the kitchen and found a fresh carafe of sangria in the fridge. They slipped the carafe past the sales guys and into the den. Sam set their glasses on the coffee table and poured. He set the carafe on a book with an Oprah sticker on its cover.

"Are you in a book club, Sparrow?"

"No."

"Come on. It gives you something to talk about. It gives you a lot to talk about."

"Reading the same books only makes you more the same. It gives you nothing to talk about at all. Reading different books is having secrets. Now there's something to talk about."

"I don't read anything. Nothing the same, nothing different. What does that make me?"

"Shallow."

"But no secrets."

"You have a secret, Sam. And you need to tell me right now."

Sam refilled their glasses to the rim. A little sangria seeped over the rim and puddled on the Oprah book. Sam leaned forward, stooping over his drink, careful not to spill, and took a sip. He held the dripping glass away from his body. Small sips.

He said, "Let's go for a walk." He looked at his watch.

Sparrow set down her glass and wiped her fingertips on the couch cushion. Sam leaned close and kissed Sparrow. The memory of her sweet taste came back to him, but he knew there had already been a last kiss, and this new kiss didn't mean anything.

Sparrow said, "Oh my."

Sam stood up. He took her hand and helped her side-step the coffee table. Sparrow held her drink away from her crinkly dress.

"Sam, why is this a good idea? The last time—"

There had already been a last time.

Sam said, "There is no this. We're not doing anything."

Don't Tell Me About Bosnia

They argued on the way to the party. Tonight, it was his driving through the snow and rain, but it was always something. Mark could feel Melanie scowling beside him. She was gripping Alina's directions, which led out of town and into the hills, and he took them there. All the twists and turns. When they reached the arch in the old stone wall, Mark slowed, and he squeezed the car into the last spot along the road. He calmed himself by counting the parked cars. The road along the stone wall was steep, and Mark set the brake hard. Rain pattered on the roof. They sat in the dark and stewed.

Ahead of them, the road made a sharp turn. It shot through the arch in the stone wall and was gone. *I'll bet that's some country*, Mark thought.

He threw his silly hat in the back seat. "I'm not wearing this."

"Wait—" Melanie had flipped down the visor mirror, and she was adding fresh umber lipstick to her mouth. Her nails were the same dark gleaming color. She daubed the color onto her lips, brought her lips together, and sealed the color.

"Come on," Mark said. "Let's get this over with."

"Be civil, okay? Shouldn't be too hard."

"Of course."

"And I suppose I should warn you: Alina is, like, really beautiful."

"So?"

"No, I mean, she's really, really, really beautiful."

"What the fuck."

"Just don't gaze at her all gaga, okay?"

"Thanks for the goddamn warning."

Mark climbed out. He helped Melanie out. Walking along the stone wall, they found the iron gate and went in. Alina's house was nestled among the blue spruce trees. Christmas lights hung from tree to tree, glowing red and warm. Woodsmoke scented the air, and the rain pattered. Mark and Melanie did not hold hands up the path. They dodged puddles and mushy snow. Melanie knocked on the oak door, and they stood apart from each other on broad flagstones.

No one came to the door. Maybe they should give up and go home. The kids were at Grandma's. Make-up sex? All their sex was make-up sex now.

"This place is amazing," Melanie said. "I love it."

The house was built out of klinker bricks, jagged and knobby. Copper trim skirted the windows. A lattice design of leaves and vines wound along the copper trim, hammered out by hand. Mark could see the tiny mallet marks.

He said, "In Bosnia I stayed in a house like this. There was—"

"Don't tell me about Bosnia." Melanie peered at the copper designs.

"For Christ's sake, Mel."

"They did all their own work, you know. Alina's an architect, and her husband—I always forget his name—anyway, he's a metal smith. Look." Melanie touched a copper sash inlaid with a flower design. The copper was shiny from so many people touching it. She smiled to herself and touched it again.

Mark found a different part of the house to look at. The jagged bricks. The hard angles. This made him feel serious and focused. It seemed familiar. He tried to make sense of the familiar feeling. *In Bosnia there was this house, and we...*

"Mark, do you get what I'm saying? They did this. All of this. Do you have any idea how much work this must have been?" Melanie was frowning at him.

"I get what you're saying, okay? Now hold still." Mark lifted his hand to Melanie's chin, and with his fingertip he daubed her lips. It was a familiar touch, but lately familiar had meant merely ordinary. Melanie didn't move, but her eyes followed the motion of Mark's hand. Her frown relaxed. Mark's fingertip came away with an umber stain. He said, "You don't need that stuff to be pretty."

Melanie's lips parted, and she took a tiny breath. She looked lovely and sad.

Mark wondered when lovely and sad had become the same.

"What time is it?" Melanie said.

"Ten o'clock. Two more hours to go."

"We are so late." She frowned again.

"Zoom zoom," Mark muttered. His eyes followed the copper trim, and he touched a dull place no one had touched before. It felt slippery and cool. He had known it would. It felt familiar. *In Bosnia, we—*

A woman—Alina?—opened the door.

"Omigod! You made it!"

Music and light and the heat burst from the doorway. Alina smiled broadly. Her dark eyes sparkled. She was beautiful. Her wavy hair fell across one side of her face, and she tucked it back and smiled. Her dark eyes took you in. She wore a black sleeveless cocktail dress. Her face was rosy, maybe from the heat. She held a martini glass. Two silver bracelets slid down her wrist as she raised her glass. She slid them back, and they jangled, light and thin.

Alina kissed Melanie, then looked at Mark and smiled. Her eyes were steady. Mark returned the look. He felt himself becoming serious, and he hoped it didn't show.

"Alina, this is my husband, Mark."

"I've heard so much about you." Alina held her martini to the side, and with her free arm she hugged Mark warmly. Her hair brushed his cheek. Her hair smelled like lavender.

"Where's the bar?" asked Mark.

"Ooh, I like him already!" Alina's arm was still around him.

Alina showed Mark and Melanie to the liquor on the sidebar, then slid away. She moved around the room, kissing, laughing, touching people on the arm.

Melanie said, "She's Romanian or something."

"She's something, alright."

Mark and Melanie each mixed a drink with Kahlua, milk, and rum. They sat on a brown leather couch and watched the other guests, none of whom Mark knew. Melanie had said there would be a lot of architect types. People were standing in clumps, talking and laughing, holding their drinks at waist level, taking it slow. None of them seemed to notice how beautiful the room was. Goddamn beautiful. The woodwork was beautiful. The copper trim around the fireplace was beautiful. The high ceiling was beautiful, with copper tiles hammered in delicate ridges.

Alina was roving with a tray of amber demitasse glasses. People made gasps of pleasure as she brought the tray to them. Alina beamed.

Melanie leaned close to Mark. "Isn't she beautiful?"

"Yeah, she's cute alright."

"No, I mean beautiful." Melanie took a gulp from her drink. "Isn't she, like, one of the most beautiful women you've ever seen? Perfect body, lush bouncy black hair. And that face. She doesn't even need makeup and she's totally stunning."

"Yeah, she's beautiful."

"Come on. Why can't you just say it? She's fucking gorgeous. You see one or two women like that in your whole life. Like your little Bosnian friend, what-was-her-name. A natural beauty."

"Lyubov," Mark muttered. It was true: Alina really was gorgeous. Lyubov was another kind of gorgeous. Lyubov. Mark hadn't thought about her in years.

"Look at Alina. Wouldn't you like to do her?"

He sipped his drink. What was the right answer? He sipped some more.

"Wouldn't you?"

"Come on, Mel."

"Come on, yourself. Be a man. I'm so sick of you hemming and hawing."

"Okay, fine. Hell yeah. I'd do her. Definitely. I'd bring her close and I'd—"

"Fuck you, Mark."

"I did Lyubov, too, you know."

"Fuck you."

He finished off his cocktail and watched Alina laughing, sipping her amber demi glass, hugging her guests. Her hair was parted on the side, and it fell over one eye, and she was tucking it back, and her beautiful face lit up, radiant. He'd do her, all right.

No, he wouldn't.

"Where's her husband?"

"He hates these things."

"So where is he?"

"In back. There's a blacksmith shop. They built that too. He likes to show it off to people who appreciate that kind of thing. You wouldn't like it."

"If you say so."

"Omigod, there's Alina's sister. I'm going to go talk to her." Melanie handed Mark her glass. Umber lipstick on the rim.

"You're going out to smoke, aren't you?"

"Where's my little purse?"

"Don't forget your little sweater."

Melanie stood, grabbed her purse and her black cardigan, and left Mark on the couch. She joined a woman across the room. The woman was no Alina, for sure. Hell no. Melanie and the woman kissed on the cheek and disappeared out the front door. The gush of cool air felt good. Mark turned to the window and watched the women wander down the path beneath the red lights. He saw a spark, then an orange glow.

Mark felt the couch shift, and he turned. Alina had sat next to him. She was holding two amber glasses. She smiled. She leaned close to him. Their arms touched.

"So."

Mark took one of the glasses. "Melanie's out with your sister."

"Oh, God, they're not smoking, are they?" Alina turned and peered out the window. Her hair fell forward, wavy and black. She tucked it back.

Mark said, "Melanie likes to be a little scandalous."

Mark and Alina stared out at the two women. Melanie saw them watching, and she turned her back.

"My sister. Good grief. Back in Ukraine, she used to—"

"I thought you were Romanian."

"Yes. It's kind of hard to explain."

"No, it isn't. Boundaries shift around."

Alina laughed.

Mark swept his arm around the room. "This place! I can't believe it. It's so beautiful."

"Thank you."

"You must love this. I mean, you have made something to love. And all this copper."

"Oh, do you do metal work?" She leaned closer.

"Hell no. I mean, no. It just reminds me. I was deployed in Bosnia, and we stayed in a house like this. That's all I'm saying. God, I miss that. You're not supposed to miss that sort of thing, but I do."

"When you're married, you're not supposed to miss anything." Alina's dark eyes were locked on his. He looked away, but he felt her eyes trying to pull him back.

He said, "I'm talking about the war. You don't miss a war."

She said, "Was there a woman?"

"Excuse me?"

"I have to ask. Was a woman involved?"

"No. I mean yes."

Mark told Alina all about Bosnia, and she looked directly at him, and she asked all the right questions about all the right things. Her eyes, and her smile, and her hair across her cheek, and her fingers tucking it back, and her other hand touching his knee, and her bracelets tinkling—Mark told her all about Bosnia. He told her about Lyubov. He told her about the stone house with copper trim and the smith's shop in back. He told her all of it, the night, the snowy rain, the warm red lights in the trees, the old stone wall, the road through the arch in the wall, the NATO white APCs rumbling past. He had been an aide on a general's staff. Never did see where those white APCs were going.

He said, "To me, it isn't really a story."

"Yes, it is. You had something."

"Excuse me?"

"You had—you have—something that no one can take from you."

"I don't have anything."

Alina laid her arm on the back of the couch. Her face rested on her arm. She closed her eyes. What was she thinking? She opened her eyes and looked back at Mark. She turned toward the window.

"They're out there a long time," Mark said.

"A second smoke?"

"Less scandalous. Just unhealthy."

She laughed, took his wrist, and squeezed. "I just love both of you!"

AT MIDNIGHT, EVERYONE GATHERED around the television in the den. The room became hot and crowded. Mark hated standing tightly in a group of people he didn't know. Melanie squeezed in and stood by Mark. She wore a plastic tiara that said 2005. She looked like a princess. Was she smiling? They watched the ball in Times Square drop, and everyone cheered and kissed. Mark and Melanie kissed. Alina's husband had come in, wearing a T-shirt and shop apron, and they kissed too. Alina smiled at her husband, and she laughed, and she held him tight. She kissed him again and rested her head against his shoulder. She closed her eyes and smiled.

Mark felt Melanie tug on his sleeve. "Why don't you just say it?"

"Would it be any better if I did?"

"You'd be more of a man if you said it. You want her."

"The hell."

"I can tell. What did you two talk about anyway? Did you talk about our kids? No, wait, I know, you told one of your goddamned Bosnia stories."

"I don't have any Bosnia stories."

"Because you were just an errand boy."

"Adjutant."

"Whatever. Did you tell her about fucking that girl? Lyubov? Lobotomy? Whatever her name was."

"No."

"You can tell Alina, but you can't tell me." Melanie began to cry.

Alina saw them. She grinned and came over and hugged them and exclaimed a Happy New Year. Her cheeks were pink. She did not let go.

Melanie smiled and looked away. "Omigod, Alina, you are always so pretty."

"Oh, no, stop that." She loosened her arm around Melanie.

"No, you're just beautiful. Your brown eyes, your sassy hair and..."

Melanie was talking too loud, and people nearby turned to listen. They looked at Alina as if to verify what Melanie had said, but then they looked back at Melanie and listened.

"And you don't even wear makeup, or just a little. I don't know. You're gorgeous. And where did you get those bracelets?"

Alina held out the bracelets. "Steve made them for me."

"Omigod, that's so nice. I just... I mean... You're just so beautiful."

"I don't know what to say."

Mark took Melanie's hand and tugged her away. "Come on."

"Ooh, Mark and Melanie!"

"What?"

"Where's your sweater? Come on."

Mark led Melanie to the car. She tugged against his hand, but when they came to the car, he kissed her long, hard, lips crushing. He pressed his hand to her breast, then slid it down to her hip. Mark knew she understood when her body softened into his.

They drove through the arch in the stone wall. Farther. Into the night. Around tight turns, fast, slippery, squealing. It was old farmland, orchards and vineyards and hay, separated by tired fences. A bridge crossed an irrigation ditch. Right-angle turns marked the corners of pastures. They went farther. In the rearview mirror, the red glow in the trees became smaller, a glimmer far away. They left the rain, and the road crossed a field under stars.

Mark pulled over as far as the car could fit on the shoulder of the road. Mark and Melanie fucked in the back seat. Mark wasn't thinking about Melanie, he wasn't thinking about Alina, he wasn't thinking about Lyubov; he tried to not think about anyone. His body was heavy against Melanie's, but she lifted and made everything light. Even that observation was too much thinking. Thinking made it more than fucking, and fucking was all it was. But it was something. He wanted them to have something.

When it was over with, Melanie cuddled against Mark and smiled. Mark fixed her tiara. Rain pattered the roof-top. The drive back to the party was long, and it was quiet, just the rain and snow and the slapping of the windshield wipers. Mark drove slowly. He didn't want to frighten Melanie. He felt bad about his rapid driving earlier. Melanie's hand gripped his hand. Darkness made it hard to find the way.

They found the red glow through the trees.

They drove through the arch, and Mark parked the car in the last space along the stone wall. Melanie fixed her umber lipstick.

"Isn't Alina beautiful? You can say it now. I won't be hurt. You can say it, and I won't be hurt."

Mark didn't say anything.

"Is she more beautiful than me? If you could have me or her, who would it be?"

Mark still didn't speak. Alina. Lyubov. Melanie. Having and wanting were two different things.

Melanie continued. "And it's not just that she's beautiful. She's so nice. I mean, she takes an interest, you know. She listens. She makes you feel close to her. You know?"

"Yeah."

"What do you mean, 'yeah?' You don't know her."

"You said, 'you know,' and I said, 'yeah.'"

"That's not what I meant. It's just something a person says."

Mark didn't respond. He listened to the rain.

IT MUST HAVE BEEN THREE O'CLOCK. Most of the guests were gone. Alina was in the backyard, sitting on a bench, facing the blacksmith shop. Her husband had fired up the furnace, and the windows of the shop glowed. Mark sat down next to Alina on the bench. Copper. Cold.

Mark looked at his glass of honey wine. A few sticky drops stuck to the sides.

"This bench is amazing."

"Steve made it."

"I can't get over this house. It's just so—" But it wasn't true anymore. Mark was completely over the house. He was tired of everything being so beautiful. The bench was hard and slippery and cold.

"I designed it, but Steve made it." She lifted her arm, slid her bracelet around her wrist, and fingered the silver designs.

Mark wondered how the house looked in the light of day. Copper in the sunshine, bright and hard to gaze upon.

"So I saw your sister and Melanie out front again."

Alina took Mark's hand and squeezed it. He squeezed back. She rested her head on his shoulder. Lavender.

"You don't have kids," he said.

"Miscarriage."

"I'm sorry."

"We'll try again."

They watched Steve at the forge. The light from the shop window glowed orange and yellow.

"So, everyone says you're beautiful." It felt silly when he said it.

"Oh, please, no." She pulled her hand back. She sounded tired.

"I mean, really beautiful." Just as silly.

"Please, no." Alina folded her arms. She let her hair fall across her face, and she did not tuck it back. Through the shop window, Steve was using tongs to take something hot and glowing out of the furnace.

After a minute, Alina said, "So what did you find up that road? That's where you went, right?"

"It was so dark, I don't know if we found anything."

"Does Melanie know about Bosnia?"

"Yes. I mean no. Not really." Mark's voice was flat.

"Why did you tell the story to me but not to her?" Alina took his hand again.

"You know what? Nothing happened in Bosnia. In fact, I don't have a Bosnia story. Not really. I have a very different story. Don't you agree?"

Alina was looking at Mark, but her hair was in the way. Mark couldn't read her.

A gust of wind shook rainwater loose from the trees. The red lights danced and sparkled, then blinked out. The shiny copper-and-brick house seemed to push against blackness. Alina nestled into Mark's side. She was somewhere. He said, "Here is what happened in Bosnia. There was this man, and there was this woman, and she was very beautiful, you know..."

Snowy Day

The morning was quiet. Annie knew why, and, rising from her bed and shuffling through the apartment, she listened to the quiet and felt the cold that could only mean one thing: a blizzard. From the kitchen window she watched the smothering snow. You could say anything in that snow, and no one would hear.

The Ukrainian girls were playing in the vacant lot again. The younger girl—braids and pink wool cap—was running a circle around the older girl—no braids, blue scarf. The older girl was pregnant, Annie was certain now, and happy. She was laughing, anyway. Too old for play, too young for anything else, the older girl stood still. The snow filled the younger girl's tracks, and she ran and threw handfuls of snow, and the older girl stood and watched and smiled, one blue mittened hand stroking her belly, the other hand batting the clouds of silent snow thrown at her. The snow gathered on her blue scarf and on her shoulders, and on her long, straight, blonde hair.

From the kitchen window, Annie couldn't hear.

Annie put a slice of bread in the toaster, warmed the skillet on the stove, melted a slice of butter, cracked an egg into it. The odor of egg got to her. She wanted to throw up. To distract herself from the odor, she looked back to the window and the girls. They were laughing. Maybe they were laughing. She really couldn't hear. Cold air slid down the pane. Her face was reflected there, last evening's makeup. She didn't want to see that.

Annie returned to the stove. She worked the spatula around the edge of the egg and slid it under, then lifted the egg onto a white plate. The yolk was broken and oozing yellow, the way her husband liked it. She set down the spatula and picked up the butter knife and buttered the toast, which had cooled. The butter was too cold to spread. It stuck in a clump on the dry, crusty slice of bread. She set the plate on the 1950s cherry-red dinette table, their wedding present to themselves, their one thing, and she tried not to think about red. It made her feel sick again. She tried not to smell the egg. She left the plate on the table.

Her little boy had gotten up. He was playing with plastic soldiers on the radiator in the main room. It was the warmest place, and it was his. He could look out the window at the vacant lot and ask about the snow, ask about the Ukrainian girls, ask about his daddy in Afghanistan. Annie knelt and kissed him and said, "Today, Mommy has to study for a test." Later, she would brush her hair and go back to her bed and read her textbook on human anatomy. The boy would climb onto her bed and plead to play outside, and she would relent, but he wouldn't last long out there, and neither would she, standing in the snow, her little boy running around her. But they would go, and he would laugh, and so would she.

She found her hairbrush on the windowsill above the radiator and said, "After I study, we can make a snowman." She sat on the end of the radiator and looked out the window, and she tugged the brush through her hair.

Her little boy played with his plastic soldiers. He made shooting sounds. He rammed the soldiers together. Annie had told him the soldiers were a present from his dad.

A man shuffled out of the bedroom. He was wearing yesterday's clothes, and he looked tired. He stopped when he saw the little boy. The little boy said, "Be quiet. She's studying."

The man went into the kitchen. Annie watched him. The man was nice enough. She was glad he was a little older, and nice, but not so nice as to be a goddamned gentleman about things, because where did that take you. The man took the plate. He rummaged through the drawers and found a fork, and he ate the egg and toast standing up. He sopped the runny yolk with a bread crust. He looked out the kitchen window. Maybe he was in a hurry. All that snow piling up, he ought to be in a hurry. He should have left already. Maybe he was looking at the pretty Ukrainian girls.

"Peter," she said. "This is my friend, Professor Johnson."

The boy did not look up. He was playing war.

The man came in and stood by the radiator. The woman set her brush on the sill. She stiffened her shoulders. She took the man's arm and led him back to the kitchen. She took his plate and put it in the sink. She scrubbed away the butter and egg smell.

The man came up behind her. He tried to hold her close, and he whispered in her ear, "Last night was real nice. And you made me breakfast—"

She said, "It was just an egg and toast, and the yolk broke." Her back was turned, and she let him hold her that way, his arms around her tummy. She rinsed the plate. His hands rose and found her breasts.

"I liked the egg runny. I liked that."

She looked out at the girls in the falling snow. Her pretty Ukrainian girls. She didn't know their names. They were close together, heads bent, telling secrets, a single cloud of breath.

"Are you free anytime soon?"

"Thomas." She looked at the sink, the water sliding away. "What are you expecting?" She held out her fingers, wet, showing her wedding ring.

He took her wet hands.

She was thinking ahead. After breakfast, she would swap the oversized Montana Guard T-shirt for her pink turtle-neck sweater and the jeans that still fit. She would take her son out to the vacant lot. She would worry about Advanced Topics in Human Anatomy and pretend to be happy while her son ran through snow as deep as his thighs. Now she let the man turn her shoulders so she was facing him, and he pulled her close, as if they were still close, as if they were anything at all. God damn it, guys were so complicated. This ought to be so simple.

She said, "Do you want another egg or not?"

"No. Listen, I know what I want—"

"I can't drink coffee anymore, but I can make some. If you have some, I'll probably have some too."

He kissed her neck. He stroked her hair. She loosened the stiff muscles in her spine and softened against him. She looked at the fridge.

"Do you see that picture? That's my husband." She mumbled the words into his shirt.

"Is that Afghanistan?"

"Actually, he's still in Kyrgyzstan. Maybe he's in Afghanistan by now. I don't know. He never writes or calls. I write pretend letters to Peter and say they're from him. Right now, I have him at a base in Kyrgyzstan. I don't even know how to spell that."

"It must be hard." He kissed her. "Actually, I feel kind of bad about this."

She pointed to another picture on the fridge. "Do you see that?"

"Yes. That's an ultrasound."

"Do I have to fucking spell it out for you?"

He stopped trying to kiss her.

"Peter," she yelled into the other room, "you need to eat something."

Explosions.

"He can't hear you."

"Yes, he can. God, don't you get anything?" She pulled away.

"I get you. I get how it is. And I get how pretty you are. I get that we had a good time. And I do feel a little sorry for you. So yes, I get it."

"Feel sorry for me? Listen! I feel sorry for you! Do you want another egg or not? With some toast and butter and apricot jam?" She started to cry, but she turned so he couldn't see. She lowered her voice. "Do you want to fuck me again? That's the thing that really hurts. I want you to fuck me again. Feel sorry for me for that."

He said nothing. Maybe he was composing a thought instead of just saying it. He was nice, but he was very complicated.

He said, "Listen. You think I don't notice these things, but you don't know. The way you look at me in class, I notice that. The way you stick around afterward, and you don't say anything, just stick around. You're sending signals you don't even know about. The sweet, dutiful mother, the army wife, come back to finish her degree. I don't care about that. I guess I care about you."

She made herself stop crying. "You think this isn't my choice? That you seduced me? Vulnerable woman has dinner and sex with her professor, wow. Well, maybe you're the one being used. Maybe I actually chose to fuck you. Maybe I even liked myself around you."

"I'm saying you're a nice lady, and you deserve to be happy."

The Ukrainian girls were gone from the vacant lot. Their footprints, close together, were filling with snow.

The man went into the bedroom for his coat and came back.

"You can call," she said. Her arms were folded for warmth. "I don't feel sorry for you. And I want you to call. I just want you to actually want to call." She loosened one arm and waved away the pictures on the refrigerator. "It's not what you think."

He wasn't looking at her. "What do I think? I think you're nice and you're—"

"I'm not nice."

"Nice enough, and pretty and sexy, and you're in a hard place. Speaking of hard places, now I need to go dig out my car."

"Thomas, are you going to call or not?"

"Sure."

"Really?"

"Sure."

"I don't believe you."

The man almost said something. He looked at her. The boy had stopped playing war. He was looking at the man. The man opened the apartment door and left.

Annie picked up her little boy, and they sat on the warm radiator and watched the man dig out his car. It was quiet today, and all she heard was her little boy's breathing, but that was enough. The man got in his car. The tailpipe gushed steam, but there was no noise. The man wouldn't call. Annie's husband wouldn't call, either. And even if he did call, would he lie to her? Annie wouldn't lie. Not anymore. Months ago, when they had stood in that vacant lot and it was so quiet that her words made the only sound, and she told him she loved him and would always be true, that had not felt like a lie. She would not lie. But he wouldn't call, no one would call, and in the quiet apartment there would be nothing to lie about. Holding her lovely boy, she would not have to puncture the silence and say she was glad for everything she had done.

Buena Vista (Part IV)

Sam led Sparrow out the front door and down the walk. Beneath those bright streetlights, you couldn't see the stars. You couldn't see the Rockies, you couldn't see the dark, hard edge of the Front Range, you couldn't see anything but here and now. The night was getting cold, and Sparrow did not have a coat. Sam pulled her close.

They got in Sam's car. They fit their sticky sangria glasses in the cupholders. The car was silent and cold, and they sat.

"People are going to talk."

"Nobody's going to talk because nobody cares. They're scripting their own—what do you call them—assignations. 'Sam and Sparrow went for a walk, ooh.' They don't know what this is about. They don't care about—"

"About what? About us?"

"They just don't care."

Sam and Sparrow sipped their sangria and drove around the development, gazing at empty identical houses until they became good and lost. And drunk. Neither spoke. The car took the wide winding streets slow and easy, which was fine with Sam. The sticky asphalt hummed. The houses were all for sale.

They stopped the car at a beige house with a porch swing. A flat green lawn had been unrolled to meet wild grass and knobby rocks and prickly pear. In the center of the grass was a stand of aspen, which never should have been planted this far out on the prairie. A sticker on the sign said Model Home. Sam and Sparrow got out.

The walkway was exposed aggregate, and the shiny lacquered pebbles made it hard for Sparrow in her heels. She leaned close. Sam felt her weight. He led her to the porch swing and sat beside her. He put his arms around her bare shoulders. Sparrow sipped the last of her sangria. Sam had finished his long ago.

The porch was small. When they pushed back the swing, it abruptly hit the house. When they swung forward, their knees bumped the wooden rail.

"That's fucked," said Sam.

"It's a faux porch. A faux swing. Bet the grass is faux too. Everything is fauxed up."

"Come on." Sam stood and took Sparrow's hand.

"No."

"Come on. Let's go inside."

"We're not supposed to be here."

They walked through the house. They took a brochure.

"Look, darling," she said. "It has one of those bonus rooms."

"Remember the apartment by City Park? We could have used a bonus room."

Sparrow held her empty glass by the tips of her fingers. She knelt and set the glass on the Pergo floor. She rubbed her fingers. "They'd sell more homes if they staged it with furniture. Make it look real. Curtains would be nice. Paintings would be nice. Charming little children running around. Anything real would be nice."

Sam took her arms, and they danced. Sparrow's heels clicked. Sam had to imagine the music, the pretty colors, the light. It was hard. He had to imagine that it was Jill wearing that crinkly black dress. They would be at a party. She would be talking to a group of women, and he would be talking to the guys, and he would spot his girl and lead her away. He remembered something, a party long ago, the light a little different, a different scent on Jill's skin. He kissed her.

He kissed Sparrow.

Sparrow's lips slid to his cheek. Her voice whispered. "What about Jill? Sam, tell me."

The book club was tomorrow. Jill and Sam would serve croissant sandwiches. Jill would wear a blue silk blouse, and Sam would volunteer to do the greasy dishes so she wouldn't have to. Jill would do all the talking, which was fine, because Sam had nothing to say.

"Jesus, Sam. What about Jill?" Sparrow kissed Sam again. "Please."

Sam held her tight and whispered. "This is what Jill likes. See, I bring her close like this." His hand tugged through Sparrow's thick black hair. Her chignon spun loose. "I kiss her, and I fuck her." He lifted Sparrow's leg over his hip and pressed his pelvis to hers. "Like this. Just—like—this."

Sparrow began to cry. Her face turned away, but Sam could smell her perfume and her warm tears. He heard the crinkling of her dress as she let her leg down.

He said, "This is just pretend."

"What the fuck is pretend about it?"

"We were never happy, Sparrow."

"We are happy now, Sam."

Sam slowed down his words. "We are only happy because we know how this ends. It's perfectly happy, but only because it doesn't mean anything."

Sparrow pulled away.

Sam said, "I'm going back. Jill and I are going to fuck like nobody's business. You and Tony too. You know you will."

Sparrow cried, and she didn't hide it anymore by turning her head away. She kicked her sangria glass into a corner of the Pergo floor, and it spun around.

Sam said, "I'm sorry. I'm very, very sorry. Damn I'm sorry. You can be mad if you want to."

"Don't tell me when to be mad."

"But it doesn't mean anything, so don't be mad."

"Don't tell me it doesn't mean anything. Damn you if you say anything else. Sometimes a girl wants a good fuck. And sometimes a fuck is anger and unhappiness as much as anything else. Sometimes a girl just wants to say, 'Fuck me,' and don't you dare tell me it doesn't mean anything."

Anasazi

Artis had been camping in the mesas before. He knew how it was. You roamed the canyons for the perfect campsite, you scrambled up the red rock, you gathered armloads of juniper sticks from the mesas and brought them down to build a fire. With any luck, your girlfriend had found an Anasazi firepit at the base of the cliffs, and you camped where people had camped for thousands of years. At night, the two of you toasted your happiness with plastic cups of wine. You ate shepherd's pie that you had wrapped in foil and cooked in the coals. As the fire died, you and your girl kept warm by dancing to music on the transistor radio, the Durango station, until the batteries froze. You slept cold, you slept close, and you woke up goddamned happy. Fresh snow on the yucca, silence in the canyon, juniper scent wafting from the cold ashes of the dead fire.

Artis said nothing when Bernice complained about the cold, the falling snow, the silence. He said nothing when Bernice complained about how he set up the gear on the picnic table, the stove on the wrong side, the water bottles too far to reach. When Artis prodded the shepherd's pie out of the coals, and the blackened foil hissed with steam that smelled like coriander and sage, and Bernice said, "I'm not eating that," Artis said nothing. Their baby, who had begun the trip happy and cooing, began to cry. Bernice held the baby against her chest, her cloud of breath close and cowering, and said, "How dare you endanger my child with all this cold?"

My child? Their child.

Artis had had enough. He kicked snow into the fire and said, "Let's go home."

But the car would not budge from the heavy snow. The tires spun in place, and the heat from the spinning tires melted the snow beneath them to an icy glaze. Artis would have to walk for help. Twenty miles to the highway. Darkness was coming. The tire tracks were filled in. Did Artis even know the way? He thought of the family who, last year, had driven into the canyons too far and gotten stuck. The dad went for help. A helicopter found the mom and kids a few days later, tired, cold, hungry. The dad never made it.

Artis packed the rucksack for the long walk. He was anxious to chase the last hopeful light of day. Then he remembered something. He said, "Listen, I think there's a cabin down in this canyon. I don't know for certain, but I'm pretty sure."

Bernice said, "And you know this how?"

"I think I remember it from a trip in college."

"Why didn't you tell me?" Bernice paced around the dead campfire. The baby slept against her chest. Snowflakes settled on the baby's wool cap.

"I wasn't sure before, but now, I'm sure."

"We're up here freezing to death, you kicked out the fire, and now you—"

He did not say, "You're supposed to enjoy nature." He did not say, "You're supposed to be goddamned happy." Instead, Artis said this: "Alice and I saw a cabin down there once." He added, "And please quiet down. You'll upset the baby."

"Oh. This is about Alice. That's why you wouldn't tell me. Did you fuck her in that cabin, Artie? Obviously, you did. I can't believe you. I don't even want to go to that cabin now."

"I'm climbing down to that cabin."

"Artie, you're going out to the highway. You'll flag down a car."

"I'm going to that cabin. I'm going to radio for help to save my wife and child."

Artis pumped his arms and legs. During the day, his gear had become wet from the snow, and now it was frozen stiff. Snow pants. Parka. Boots. Mittens. Cap. A scarf Bernice had knitted for him out of alpaca wool.

Bernice continued to pace around the dead firepit. "Don't take anything off. That's what happens, so they say. You remember that family? The dad took off his clothes. They found his body by following a trail of discarded clothes."

"I think I'll keep my clothes on."

"You're sure there's a cabin? Don't leave me up here while you look for a cabin you vaguely recall fucking your girlfriend in."

"I'm sure there's a cabin, with a generator and a radio."

"At first you didn't remember, then you weren't sure, and then you were quite sure, and now you're so precisely sure that you even remember a radio?"

"Yes."

"It's all coming back to you. Oh, Artie, yes, yes."

"You know, the Anasazi culture collapsed while they quarrelled over petty stuff. With the last of their warmth, they argued. Whether to rinse out the wine from the plastic cups before they stacked them. Whether to place them here or there. On their picnic table. Beside their hogan."

"Did you fuck her in the night? Did you fuck her in the morning?"

"They must have felt the blood and heat under their skin. Did they even have plastic cups in those days?"

Artis stepped close enough to smell his baby and feel the warmth. The snowflakes were melting on the baby's cap. Artis and Bernice were supposed to be happy. This was the mesas. This was the canyons. He knew how it was supposed to be.

He put on the rucksack. He said, "Don't sleep in the car. It's warmer in the tent. I can't explain why, but it's absolutely true. Nothing but the cold air under the car."

He left Bernice and the baby in the cold and snow, and he picked his steps down the steep wash that led into the canyon and the layers of red rock. The exposed roots of juniper were the only handholds. Farther down, the juniper thinned, and the red rock was bare. In the most distant light, he thought he could see a cabin's tin roof through the cottonwoods. He was sure of it. The cabin. There had been dancing. Blood and heat rushed to his skin. He remembered! Every slippery step took him closer. He was climbing alone, quietly, remembering how it was.

Deep into the canyon, he found aspen trees clinging to cracks in the rock. The snow slid away as he climbed among the rocks. Far above, he saw Bernice with the baby, peering over the edge. She didn't seem to see him. Artis climbed through the aspens, and he couldn't see her anymore. It was quiet. Don't fall, he told himself. He was working up a sweat. He loosened the alpaca scarf, and when it slipped away, he let it drop. Did Bernice see that?

It was a difficult trail through the aspens, if it qualified as a trail at all, and Artis knew he would never be able to climb back up to the mesa. He had better be right about this cabin. He thought of the old times, dancing with Alice to the transistor radio. The memory took away the cold and pain, but he forced himself to stop thinking of the old times, because he needed to feel pain to survive. He thought about Bernice. He thought about his baby. He tripped on the aspen roots and walked. This wasn't a trail. It was running away.

The pitch of the canyon eased to jumbled rock. Aspens gave way to cottonwoods. Artis climbed over rocks mounded with snow. Sweat and snow soaked his boots. The cold air made his face ache. His hands went numb. His breath froze around his mouth. Tears froze at the corners of his eyes.

Bernice had devised hand signals. Artis was supposed to stop now and then, keeping her posted as he worked down the canyon. Every move, keep her posted.

The hell he would.

Artis and Alice had danced in the cabin. What was the signal for dancing? There wasn't one. Artis was dancing in the snow now. He made footprints all around. He took off his coat for dancing. His cap and mittens too. The trail had flattened out. It was the bottom of the canyon, a bed of smooth rocks where the creek had run dry. The cliffs blocked the sun, and the cottonwoods were stunted things, and it was cold as hell. Snow matted the yuccas. Perfect quiet. Gray light. Artis finished dancing. He picked up his clothes and walked down the creek bed easy as taking a stroll.

He found the cabin on a high bank above the creek bed. The cabin was locked, but he found the key hidden under a shingle by the door, exactly where they had found it last time. They had laughed about it then. He laughed about it now.

The cabin consisted of a big room—for dancing, Artis told himself—and a bunkroom in back. For fucking. Enough wood for a few fires. Artis made a fire, but the smoke was slow to draw because of the cold. The cabin filled with smoke. The iron stove groaned from the heat, and finally it began to draw. Artis went outside to start the generator, but the noise was too much, and he turned it off. They had turned it off ten years ago for the same reason. Artis and Alice dancing! To come back to the mesas and see the crisp starlight above the black of the canyon walls, and to dance—the memory hurtled back! Artis went inside. Clumsy boots scraped a tired floor.

He lay on a bunk in the back room and shut his eyes. In his mind he heard Bach. The radio had died, country music from Durango, and Alice had begun whistling Bach as Artis held her, and spun her, and gathered her again. Bach wrote dances. Alice told him so. *Allemande. Gigue. Menuet. Sarabande.* He remembered the words. He wanted to tell Bernice.

He wanted to say he longed for happiness, that they, too, could be this happy way. Bernice could come to the cabin. Their baby would stay warm by the fire. The dishes would be neatly put away. He would whistle the music, and they would dance. She would come to him, fly over the snow to him. He would wait for them. He who could as easily fly away.

ARTIS STOOD OUTSIDE as the morning sun cracked the top of the canyon. He was cold and perfect and alone. His breath tinkled as it froze. He heard another noise and saw Bernice sloughing down the dry creek bed. She carried the baby on her back, and she swung her arms wide as she fought for footing in the snow. She was slipping and sliding from going too fast. Her hot breath floated, then froze, then fell from the air.

Bernice dragged up to Artis. She was panting. She swung the baby carrier off her back. Her sweat had frozen into her hair. Artis was glad they were alive. He was glad they had come. He didn't say anything. He took the baby.

Bernice said, "You threw away the scarf. I saw you."

He said, "It fell."

She said, "Why didn't you signal us?"

He said, "I did signal you. I made a fire. I wanted you here. Goddamn you, I wanted you here. Why would I want anyone else? Or anything else. Does it matter? You came. You saw the fire, and you came."

Bernice was still panting. She said, "Do you know how much work that was? Carrying the baby. We could have been killed."

"Yes."

"Well, you didn't say anything about it. You could have met me where the trail came down to the creek."

"You know, the Anasazi used to—"

"This where you fucked her, Artie?"

"Does it matter?"

"We froze in that car, you know."

"I told you not to sleep in the car."

Artis went in. He set the baby on a bottom bunk, wrapped in everything he could find, and he stoked the fire. He went out to start the generator while Bernice tinkered with the CB radio. Artis came back in, but only because it was preferable to the racket of the generator outside. Bernice was talking on the radio. Artis didn't say anything. He wanted to say this: joy required too much effort to imagine. He took his baby from the bunk and sat by the woodstove and wept tears that did not freeze. His face felt hot. Tonight, he would sleep with his memories. All the times they had sat on the bare rocks on top of the mesas and waited for the sunset, glad to wait forever, Artis and Bernice, keeping each other warm and happy for it—memories now.

THE SNOWMOBILES CAME THE NEXT DAY. Park Service rangers: two crewcut men and a young woman with her hair in a long braid. Artis asked them about Alice. Maybe they remembered her; she had worked as a summer ranger during college. They said they did not remember her. It was too late in the day to reminisce. Too cold. They unloaded their packs and headed for the cabin.

Bernice was putting the cabin in order. Stock the wood bin, wipe down the kitchenette, sweep the porch. The baby slept on Bernice's back as she moved about the porch with a broom. The rangers said hello to Bernice, stomped the snow from their boots, and went inside. Bernice swept the snow away.

She paused the sweeping and stared at the snowmobiles. "How are we all going to fit on those?"

"You ride on the back and hold onto the driver, like on a motorcycle."

"What about the baby?"

"On your back, I suppose. Or on my back. I don't know."

"That's too dangerous."

"No, this, this, this, is too dangerous." Artis pointed to everything. The cabin, the canyon walls, the graying sky. If he could have pointed to cold, the goddamned cold, he would have pointed to it, but how did you point to something you felt all the way to your bones?

At night they danced to the rangers' transistor radio. Country music. Durango station. The rangers knew all the tunes. They had plenty of batteries! Bernice and the ranger woman took turns dancing with the ranger men. Bernice smiled and laughed. Artis held his warm, quiet baby, and he watched Bernice, and he watched the ranger woman, who had loosened her long braid, and he didn't dance with anyone.

The rangers let Artis and Bernice have the bunkroom. For fucking. But Artis and Bernice didn't fuck. They could have fucked. They could have moved the sleeping baby out of the way, easy, and fucked. They didn't. Artis and Bernice each took a bunk, Bernice with the baby, Artis alone. He turned his back. He listened to the night. He felt his own warmth. He thought of everything at once, too much to think about, everything in his life that could have been different. Smells and music and heat. He thought of Bernice. He thought of Alice.

From the other bunk, Bernice said, "I'm not going on those snowmobiles. I'm not putting my baby on one of those things."

"What choice do you have?"

"I'm not doing it."

Artis lay still and thought about warmth. He said, "Can we please not talk. I'm trying to think."

"About all your poor little problems. Your only problem is to take care of us."

"That's the problem I'm thinking about."

The Anasazi had one big problem. They tried to solve all the little ones.

IN THE MORNING, THE RANGERS were sweeping the fresh snow off the snowmobiles. They were packing away their gear.

It was going to be a bright sunny day, and the sun would rise high enough to reach the canyon floor, but not yet, and it was still very cold. For now, the canyon held only the gray light of shadows. The rangers were fiddling with the choke settings on their machines. The snowmobiles were bright yellow in the gray light.

Artis stepped from the cabin porch, walked over to the rangers, and said, "Go."

"What?"

"You heard me. Go. Leave. Depart. Véte. Scram."

"You'll die out here."

"Go. Go the hell away."

The rangers looked at each other. They got on their snowmobiles and started up their angry noise.

The snowmobiles went off a ways. The last driver looked back. He said, "It's twenty fucking miles, pal." He said, "The thing is, you're not the first guy to be unhappy. We see this all the time. We know how it is." The snowmobiles went away, and the canyon went quiet. The canyon went cold.

Artis went inside to his life.

Bernice was seated by the woodstove. She was breastfeeding the baby. She said, "Artie, we don't—"

"Don't say anything. Dear god, please don't say anything. Tidy up if you want something to do."

"Don't tell me what to do."

"Sorry."

She said, "You know what I think? We don't have a happily-ever-after. That's what you want, isn't it? That's what you think about, isn't it? Alice and you living happily ever after. Well, you and I don't have a happily-ever-after."

The baby began to cry. Bernice helped the baby regain her breast. The baby latched on.

"Yes, we do," Artis said. "We have this here right now. Completely and utterly for each other. Stuck with each other is more like it, but we don't have to see it that way."

Bernice said, "You know what? You don't regret the things you've done. You don't even regret the things you haven't done. You regret the things to come. The things with me."

Artis felt nothing and said, "I don't regret anything at all."

Night came. They cooked oatmeal, the last of their food, and sat by the fire. They drank warm water because they were out of tea. The cabin had enough cheap juniper wood for maybe one or two more days.

Bernice said, "Artie, do you remember the stadium?"

"The stadium?"

"Mile High Stadium? The man at the Broncos game? The drunk man behind us who said something to me. You didn't fight him. You didn't fight for me. That little incident told me everything I needed to know. I should have paid more attention."

"You would have found the fighting just as distasteful."

"That's not the point. I'm not Alice. You wanted Alice. You would have fought for Alice. I can't be your Alice." Bernice began to cry.

"The point is I'll fight for you now."

"But there's not anyone here."

"To call you a bitch? So I can kick his ass? We can get the snowmobilers back here…"

"You'd like that, wouldn't you. That was a lovely girl with the long braid. One thing I don't understand, though. Artie, tell me this. Why didn't you stay with Alice?"

Artis didn't know. He and Alice had not managed to secure their own happily-ever-after. He didn't know. He only knew that by the end, they were fighting. He said, "She wanted coasters on the coffee table."

"Coasters are a good idea, Artie."

"The coffee table was boards and cinder blocks. College stuff."

"So come on. What happened?"

"No more dancing. That's what happened. We got on with living."

Bernice stared at him. She didn't understand.

Artis got up from the fire.

Bernice said, "Wait. You left your glass."

She indicated with her eyes. The glass was on the floor.

Artis paused. He could pick up that goddamned glass. Or he could leave it on the floor. When you were dying in the cold, why did things have proper places anymore? He put it here, she put it there. This was their dance. Your certain way was not mine.

Don't Say Anything

One month alone, and Jesse was still getting used to things. He was filling a saucepan for tea—Anna hadn't let him take the kettle—and when he touched the stove and the faucet at the same time, he got an electrical jolt across his body. His arm jerked back, and the saucepan flew off the stove and clanged on the kitchen floor. The old heap must have been ungrounded. Jesse swore. He curled into a corner of the kitchen floor and rubbed his aching arm. His heart thumped a fast, funny beat.

Anna and Henry were outside, playing in the vacant lot. Through the window, Jesse could hear their laughter as they, unaware of his accident, chased a neighbor's cat around. Anna had brought Henry's overnight bag and his teddy bear, and now Jesse wished Anna would say her goodbyes and leave. Get on with things, this new way, apart from each other. The oven contained a cake for Henry's birthday, and Jesse figured that he and Henry would eat it all themselves.

Jesse had never baked a cake before, and the kitchen smelled surprisingly good, but he didn't want to touch the oven again. How to get the cake out? He didn't want another shock.

Outside Jesse's window, a young woman came down the fire escape. Jesse saw her bare feet picking spots on the iron grate. The woman peeked in the window, her fingers folding around the sash. She said she lived upstairs. She had heard all the clatter. Was anything wrong?

Jesse sat up from the floor and knelt, still gripping his arm. The woman climbed in the window.

She helped him wipe the water off the floor. She wore a sundress, yellow with red polka dots. The hem of her dress skimmed the wet floor as she worked. Her feet left small wet prints on the old linoleum. She tucked back her hair, looked up from the puddle of water, and said her name was Jessie. Same as his. They laughed about that. She wiped the floor.

She asked, "So, what's your major?" She looked at Jesse and waited for his answer. She had beautiful brown eyes.

Jesse shook his head and held up his hand. "Uh, parenting."

"You don't go to the U?"

"No, but obviously you do."

The young woman gave up a smile. She stood, gathered the ends of her skirt, and climbed out the window to the fire escape. Her arched feet nimbled over the dish of cat food on the landing, and she was gone. Jesse's hands trembled. He left the saucepan in the sink. He didn't want tea anymore. He was shaking. His body remembered the stove.

From the window, Jesse watched Anna and Henry chasing the cat in wide circles in the grass. The sun cast long shadows across the vacant lot. Fairy rings had sprouted in the open spaces, but college students had worn a path among them. Jesse saw the sunset turning pink, and he heard his son's laughter, and Anna's voice giving encouragement, and from the upstairs apartment window he heard dishwater splashing, and the girl, Jessie, singing a tune, "One, two, three, four, tell me that you love me more..." From another window came the sounds of a couple having sex. Jesse closed his eyes for five long seconds. His heart still rattled about.

Wearing a hot-mitt and using just one hand so as not to complete a circuit through his body, Jesse opened the oven and took out the cake. His hands were shaking as he spread the can of green frosting on the cake top. Henry had asked for green. The frosting melted on the hot cake, pooling along the edge of the pan. Should have let it cool. Anna would remark about that. She should have left already. He stuck four candles in the cake. Bought them himself. He had never bought birthday candles before. He didn't know where to put the box of extra candles. Hadn't thought of that. A drawer? Above the stove? Fucking stove.

Matches. He had forgotten matches. The neighbor, Jessie, maybe she had some. He wiped his hands on a towel, lifted the cake, and climbed out to the fire escape landing. Climbing the stairs, he heard Jessie on the telephone, her voice through her kitchen window, talking and laughing, "Dude, that's so awesome!"

Never mind.

Jesse turned back, stepped over the dish of cat food, and carried the unlit birthday cake down the iron stairs to his wife and son.

Long light combed through the grass. It was end-of-summer light. End-of-a-good-day light. The sun filled the cottonwood leaves with light, and the empty lot glowed with pink light through the leaves. Jesse was happy to have this light. Every night, sitting on his fire escape and watching the pink light, he didn't have to explain anything to anyone, which meant he didn't explain anything hurtful or bad. The night would come, hard and alone, but evening was a beautiful time if you could stand the cold. It was always cold. It was Missoula, the northern Rockies, and it was always cold in the evening. You wore a sweater. Anna was wearing a blue sweater. She looked good in a sweater.

Jesse's little boy was chasing the cat around the lot. Anna sat at a picnic table that the college students had dragged over from a city park. The long light of a Montana summer evening made Anna's skin look pink and warm. She was drinking wine from one of Jesse's plastic cups. She frowned as Jesse laid the cake on the table.

"It's not lit," Anna said in her slow, sleepy voice. She wasn't mad.

"I don't have matches."

"Jesus, Jess." Anna dug through her purse and found a lighter.

"What the fuck," Jesse said.

"None of your business," she said.

"So if my son starts smoking and dies of cancer, can I never forgive you?"

Jesse took the lighter and tried to light the candles on the cake. His hands still shook, and the flame danced around the wick. "Uh, I took a little jolt from the stove."

"The stove? What about Henry?"

"He'll be fine as long as he's not grounded when he touches it."

"Oh good, explain that to a four-year-old."

"The knobs are just his height too. It's a funky old—"

"I don't like it. I don't like any of this," Anna said.

"He likes it. I like it. He likes the fire escape and the Murphy bed, and he likes that stray kitty. Besides, it's only for a while."

"Until what."

"Until I-don't-know. Heck, I haven't even told you about the airshaft. See, there's this little door that—"

"No." Anna put her hands over her face.

"I'm sorry, Anna."

"Sorry about what, Jess?"

Jesse sat at the picnic table. Henry ran over and sat in his lap. They sang Happy Birthday and ate warm pieces of cake. Green frosting stuck on their fingers. Jesse's heart slowed to a placid pace.

Henry asked why he was getting this second birthday cake. Was he another year old?

Anna stepped away from the table. Her face shone in the light. Her shoulders were tight. Her jaw was tight. She must have been cold. Jesse scooted from under Henry's weight and went over to stand by Anna.

Anna stared into the pink sun, then she looked down. Her sleepy voice said, "He thinks I'm spending the night too."

"You didn't tell him?"

"He wouldn't come if he knew otherwise."

"What the fuck. This is my night. My first night. His and mine."

"There'll be hitches. It's okay. I can take him home. I got nothing else to do."

They walked farther into the grass and into the light. It was cold. Arms touching.

"Damn it, Anna. This is a fucking undermine."

"Look, I'll stay and tuck him in. When he's asleep, I'll leave. We'll put him in the bed and hope he doesn't wander out and touch the stove or fall down the airshaft or climb the fire escape. Happy now?"

"Happy?"

"And then I'll go, okay?" Anna started to cry but the muscles in her face fought it back.

Behind them came a clatter. The neighbor girl, Jessie, stood on the fire escape. She was putting out a fresh bowl for the cat. She wore an Icelandic sweater over her sundress. It was cold in Missoula. She understood this. She was smoking a cigarette on her landing. She did have matches.

"Look at the light." Jesse pointed at the apartments, the sun still catching the second and third floors. He was thinking about the light on the girl's long, loose hair.

Anna's voice. "So, Jess, I was thinking…"

"What?"

"About his preschool…"

"Sure. But just look at the sunlight. It's only for a moment."

"Listen to me."

Jesse didn't listen. He ran back to the picnic table and played with his little boy. Crumbs and frosting smeared Henry's face, and Jesse didn't even bother to clean him up. They chased the cat. The cat was young and playful, and it stayed close to them, but when Henry and Jesse began chasing each other the cat lost interest, ran through the bushes, and was gone. No matter. Jesse picked up his boy and swung him around and around, matting down the grass.

Two girls came around the front of the apartments and across the worn path. One of them stepped off the path and bent over a fairy ring, picking flowers with her right hand, while her left hand held back her hair. The other girl knelt beside her and picked flowers too. The girls stood close, touching. Each girl held a fist of weedy flowers and tucked them into the other's hair. They climbed up three flights of the fire escape and into the girl named Jessie's window.

Anna stepped up to Jesse and Henry. She snared Henry in her arms. "Seems to be a lot of pretty co-eds around here." She wiped Henry's face with a cloth. She looked tired. She still had her ring on. Her fingers looked old.

Henry said, "What's a co-ed, mommy?"

Anna said, "Um, I don't know, a girl."

"That's silly."

Jesse said, "Your mom was a co-ed."

Anna kicked Jesse.

"A what?"

"A beautiful co-ed."

Anna laughed and rolled her eyes. She took the wine bottle and refilled her plastic cup. Jesse sat with Anna on the picnic table and drank wine and watched Henry expend his playful energy running around the vacant lot. Get him good and tired before bed.

Henry stopped and watched them. Puzzled.

Jesse said, "Co-ed is short for co-educational."

Henry cackled but surely did not understand. This would be all right. But it would not be all right. That's what the marriage counselor had warned. It would not be all right, but what could you do? Poor Henry.

Jesse led Anna and Henry in. They climbed the fire escape, left the cake and the wine on the fire escape landing, and entered through the window. Inside, while Anna tidied up the kitchen, Jesse tried to demonstrate that he could get it right: changing Henry into pajamas, brushing his teeth, helping him go pee, singing all the right songs. Henry found the airshaft's little door right away, but Jesse blocked it with the heaviest box he could find. Good thing he hadn't unpacked the boxes. Henry bounced on the bed and asked about his mom. Jesse said she was cleaning dishes.

"This is a mess," she yelled in. "You need some paper for the cabinets and drawers. You just do."

Henry kept bouncing on the bed.

Anna came into the main room. Jesse and Henry began a tug-of-war with the Murphy bed, pushing and pulling the bed into the wall and out again.

"He'll squish his fingers!"

"Everyone likes it."

"Everyone? I didn't know you had so many friends in bed."

"Knock it off, Anna."

A voice came from the kitchen. The girl, Jessie, had come into Jesse's apartment from the fire escape. She peeked around the corner, smiled, and held up Jesse's serving spoon inquiringly. Then she was gone. Scampered away. Her footsteps made little pings on the iron landing.

Anna said, "What was that all about?"

Jesse opened his mouth to say something, but there were no words. It was nothing, a neighbor girl borrowing a serving spoon, and there were no words for something when it was nothing. He held his son tight and rolled on his back.

"Your concubine?"

"I think her name's Jessie. She goes to the U and—"

"What the fuck is this place?"

"Well, there's a ton of students, okay? She's borrowing a spoon. A spoon, Anna. She's probably getting stoned with her friends, watching TV, munching Häagen Daz, getting fat."

"She's beautiful."

"I guess." Jesse and Henry rolled the other way.

"Don't 'I guess' me. You know it. How many other hotties live here?"

"What's a hottie, Dad?"

"Will you just get on with things? I'll wait outside." Jesse climbed off the bed, into the kitchen, and out to the fire escape. He drank wine from the bottle and dangled his legs into the last violet light before dark. He scooped out cake with his fingers.

The key to happiness was the light. The last light. It was private, and he wished Anna would go, so the light would stay private. She was inside, putting Henry down, and he wished to sit alone and say nothing and watch the light's slender swords slide between the highest cottonwood leaves, longer, until the night allowed the dark to stay. Loneliness would set in, but Anna would be somewhere else. He could handle loneliness alone. With her it would be too much to bear. He closed his eyes.

They had been fixing up a rough timber house on five acres along the Clark Fork. It backed against the river. Half their property was flooded in the spring, but the house was above the water line, and it was perfect. Swallows nested in the eaves, and at night they circled over the water. Every night, Jesse drank wine in the kitchen and listened to the river whispering. Through the small kitchen window, he watched the swallows fly their long circles. The low sunlight made the fog pink and glowing, and the window became a little box of color, and Jesse swore on the light through that small window. He was going to replace that window with something big. Then Anna came back from her shift at the hospital. Every night, they sat in their kitchen and gazed at the small window and thought different thoughts. They fought about money and time, and after Anna had stormed off, Jesse sat in the long slow fading light and knew it was over. When the darkness was so complete that the window shrank to nothing, Jesse wandered into the bedroom and the incandescent light. Anna busied herself knitting. Jesse dreamed of a happier time. He closed his eyes to the artificial light and dreamed of it hard. He couldn't tell her. There wasn't supposed to be a time happier than this.

A police car zoomed down the avenue. Everything that was wrong seemed far away.

The two girls who had visited Jessie were sitting at the picnic table in the dark, kicking each other's feet. Then it was time to go. The girls leaned close and walked the worn path. Their arms brushed. Intimacy became a game, one of them wrestling and tugging and falling into the other, then giggling and helping her up and smoothing her long hair, and then it was over. They got to the sidewalk. They didn't hug. One girl ran, her hair lifting back. The other girl ran too, far from this, her fingers clenched around her hair.

Anna came out. The fire escape rang with her steps. She took the bottle of wine from Jesse and poured two cups, and together they sat on the fire escape and drank the wine. Someone in the apartments was playing Bob Marley.

Anna said, "I should go."

"Yeah."

Anna looked at the wine bottle. "I have to drive. That fucking house."

"You gonna sell it?"

"Did Henry tell you we saw a cougar? Your little boy saw a cougar. I didn't believe it until I went out there and saw the tracks in the sand by the swing set."

Jesse poured himself more wine.

"It's going to be so dark. I hate that. I hate that house. I hate it out there."

"You should get a gun."

"Fuck you."

"Just be civil. This is good wine. Like in Taos. Remember?"

"Yeah." She poured another cup.

"So, you were saying about his preschool…"

"Shut up about his preschool. I'll just send you the bill."

They ate cake. They drank wine. It was cold, and they sat close together.

Anna said, "What the hell are you going to do, Jesse?"

"You know. This is what I do."

"And it's fucked."

"I'm the happiest I've ever been."

"Fuck you." She leaned against him.

Her arm felt warm against his, and it felt familiar, and her shoulder fit the way it always did, and her sweater hugged her body the same as always too. Jesse put his arm around her, and her shoulders tensed, then gave, and her head rested on his chest. She was close and warm. She didn't say anything.

The purple sky of a long northern summer evening held out.

They leaned close and kissed. He pushed back her hair.

"Jesse."

"No. No. Don't say anything."

They fucked like old times. They moved Henry's little body to the Goodwill sofa, and they fucked on the bed that folded into a wall. Fucking was always something good they had. They knew how to be tender. Maybe they were used to being cruel, but they put that aside, and they spent the little tenderness they had left. They knew how to please each other decently. The right touches down the muscles along the spine. Finding the contours of the hip bones and pressing together. And all the while, Jesse knew there would be another woman someday, but there would never be Anna. There would never be this again. Did Anna know it too? You didn't ask those things. They nestled together long after any hope was left, but Montana summer nights did not last long, and dawn was already seeping into the room, and Anna's wavy hair was tangled, and she pushed it back with the heel of her palm and squinted at the bluing sky. They woke up adrift in the bed. The bed had rolled into the center of the room.

Jesse and Anna didn't say anything. A long time ago, words had broken the ice, opened the heart. Standing beneath aspens on a hike in Taos, Jesse had told her, "You are so beautiful." She had said, "No, you're beautiful." But this time, there would not be words. There was nothing to explain. When the only choice lay in deciding who would break whose heart, you didn't say anything.

It was Jesse's turn. He got up. The air against his skin felt cold. The wall hummed with water in the pipes. Someone was singing and taking a bath. You could hear it through the airshaft, a Joni Mitchell tune. Jesse looked at Anna. She looked at him the way she always did in the morning, a smile, only today it was wry and pained.

Jesse went to the window. There was the long, lovely Montana sunlight, from the east this time, the shadows slicing the other way. Last week he had seen a coyote on its morning round. The fairy rings, heavy with dew, slumped over. The two girls were in the lot again. They sat on the cold, wet edge of the picnic table, shoulders touching. They each wore a T-shirt and shorts, and they must have been cold. Later, they would leave, and Henry and Jesse would play in the grass. Hide and seek and fairy villages. They'd have a picnic. Then the long shadows Jesse loved best would collapse across the grass, and Anna would come back to pick up Henry, and Jesse would watch the sunset alone and make his old life go far away. He turned.

"This is my time," he said. "So go."

"I am going. You don't tell me." Anna shoved her hair back and looked around the bed for her clothes.

"So do it, then."

"I am," she yelled.

"Shh."

Henry began to stir.

"He can't hear me." She gathered up her things, shuffled to the bathroom.

"Shh… just shh." Jesse looked away. Don't say anything. Make it hurt less. When you break a heart, don't say a thing. Jesse put on shorts and a yellow New Mexico T-shirt. Anna emerged from the bathroom and left quietly. The front door made a soft click.

As the sunrise lit up the room, the girl's singing floated from the airshaft. A new tune that Jesse did not know. Henry woke up, and he and Jesse played on the bed. For breakfast, Jesse served leftover cake. Henry knelt on a chair at the table and ate two pieces of cake. Small pieces. The bare, bright light cut through the trees on the eastern side of the lot. The bare light promised a hot day.

A girl passed the window. Those slender feet again. It was Jessie. She wore a pink T-shirt and a printed Indian skirt. Wet hair. She peeked in, her fingers on the sash.

"Jesse? Are you in there?"

"Good morning, Jessie. This is my son, Henry."

Jessie peeked into the main room and smiled sweetly at the boy. Henry did not look up from his cake.

"Hey, Henry. My name's Jessie too." She turned. "I brought back your serving spoon. I'm sorry. I'm still getting set up."

"Me too."

She leaned against the kitchen counter. "Have you seen my kitty? He didn't come in last night."

"Not since then. Do you want some breakfast? We have lots of cake."

"Oh, I don't know." The girl looked down. She fidgeted her bare feet. She finger-combed her wet hair.

"Please. I mean, we have a lot of cake."

"Okay…"

"Don't say anything. Just eat."

She smiled. She looked down again, but only for a moment. She looked at Jesse, resting her eyes there, and she smiled. Jesse didn't know what to say. He liked her, but come on… he had ten years on her. He wanted to tell her there would be sorrow, hope and abundant sorrow, and someday she would understand. But not today. He wanted to tell her about the light, the beautiful light in the evening, but he did not. He didn't want words for anything, gazing at the pretty girl who smiled back at him for the longest time. She was not shy, and she kept combing her fingers through her wet hair, and her bare wet feet shifted around, and her gaze was solid on his eyes—until she rested her wet hand on that funky old stove and it happened, the electricity, 220 volts, hard and sharp, seized her muscles and shook her, and she twisted away.

She cried.

The girl Jessie sunk down, her body balling up, her skirt sticking to her wet legs. She was trembling from her fingertips to her spine.

Jesse knelt and held her.

Henry came running as far as the doorway and watched.

"Stay back!" Jesse yelled. He held the wet barefoot girl and stroked her wet hair, and it took all his strength to say, "Shh." His breath was spent and dry when he tried to say, "The light in the evening… the long shafts…" And when the girl looked up at him confused as a child, Jesse didn't have enough breath to whisper, "Don't say anything."

Buena Vista (Part V)

Sam and Sparrow pushed the porch swing back. Thump. They let it slide forward, and Sparrow notched her high heels against the porch rail. They pushed the swing back again. Thump.

"Do you think we could have been happy, Sam? A place like this. We could have forged ahead. Worked it out. We wanted it. You know we wanted it, Sam."

"That's the problem, though. We were always wanting. Jill and I don't want anything. I really don't want anything."

"So you're saying that you have everything you want? Right."

He put his arm around her. She was warm, and her perfume was pressed into his shirt. But he didn't care. He said, "No. I did not say that. You're a lovely woman, Sparrow, and I said that I don't want anything."

There Is No Leslie Forever

The girl on Jordan's bed rustled and stirred. I watched over her. I found a place to sit beside her on the bed, and her hand found mine, an accidental touch, and if I did not make the slightest move, her hand would stay with mine. The girl whimpered in her sleep. Maybe she was having a bad dream, but I didn't know. What scared a sleeping girl?

She opened her eyes. She blinked. She looked around. Her eyes took in Jordan's blanket tucked beneath her cheek, took in Jordan's rug and all the things she'd scattered there, his LPs, his weed, his tequila. She looked at Jordan's framed photo next to the bed. Who the hell kept a framed photo of himself? Jordan did. The fucker. The girl saw me beside her, whoever I was, and she saw where her hand lay on mine, and she settled her gaze beyond me, maybe on the window, where the wind and snow were laying a feast. The girl closed her eyes and shed a tear. What had she seen that was so painful? She pulled back her hand.

I stroked her hair. I thought she would like that. Two years of college, I had never been so close to a girl. Her hair shone in the dark, shone in the light from the window, the lamps along the pathway, the pathway smothered under snow. I stroked the girl's golden hair.

The girl said, "Goddamn it."

I leaned down and kissed her cheek. I had never been so close to a girl. She opened her eyes, but she wasn't looking at me.

She buried her face and muttered into the pillow, "You're not Jordan."

I said, "I'm his roommate. Jordan's gone. What's your name?"

"Shush."

"You want some water?"

"No."

I said, "My name is Ri—"

"Shush." She rolled onto her back, reached her arms up, and wrapped them around my neck. I felt my weight pulled onto her. Her sweater was soft. She kissed me. Her eyes were closed, a fact I knew because mine were open.

I said, "We don't have to do this."

She said, "Yes, we do." She kissed me again.

I stroked her hair from her face. I called her "baby." I breathed the word into her marvelous, shiny, silky hair.

She said, "Dude, did your dick freeze off or something?"

"What?"

"Perhaps we can get on with it."

I didn't know what to do. She pushed me aside and took off her jeans and underwear. I took off mine. We kissed. She took off her sweater and her turtleneck and her bra. I took off my flannel shirt. We got under the blanket. Jordan's blanket. When our bodies slid together, they were cold. We didn't say anything about that. A gust of wind roared, then went silent. The lack of talking made me nervous enough to say something, say anything. I said, "It's Jordan's bed." It was a stupid thing to say, so I said, "He's out with Caitlin Michaels." That didn't quite get it either, so I added, "This time."

The girl whispered, "Jordan's a fairy. That's why he gets all those dates."

She pulled me tighter. Hard to miss the scent of flowers, my face buried in her hair.

I said, "My sister's a junior. Maybe you know her. She—"

"Shut up already." The girl kissed me hard, like a punch to the lips. I pressed against her. This was how you did it? I didn't know. She wrapped her legs around my hips, reached down, helped me stick it in. We did the clumsiest thing. In and out. I heard voices beyond the door—the guys were picking up bottles in the suite before the RA came around. They cursed each other. They cursed Jordan. The girl and I pressed against each other, again and again. Then I felt a rush of heat, but I slipped out, and I shot my wad onto Jordan's blanket. I wondered if this still counted as having done it with a girl. Jordan could tell me. But he would not find out about this, because I would clean his blanket before he got back. Fucker. The girl slid away from me and turned her face.

The deed was done, but I would not look at it. I gazed out the window. Cold air dripped down the glass. My reflection gazed back at me, but I saw through it to the snow that smothered everything: the quad, the buildings, the trees. Everything was soft, round lumps, silent, made nameless from the snow. Not a single footprint down a single path.

Jordan was out there. Caitlin Michaels was out there. She and Jordan were at the hotel for the Theta winter ball. Caitlin had no idea what she was in for. Maybe she did. Jordan was probably getting them a room for the night. Jordan and me, the two studs.

Get you some?

Yep, you?

I got mine.

Sweet!

Long veins of frost had spread across the inside of the window. It was our own sweat, our own breath, condensed and frozen to the glass. Guess that's what happened when you got hot-and-heavy on a cold night. We could have scratched our names into the frost with our fingernails. But I didn't know her name. Jordan would have known her name. I turned to the girl. The girl's hair shone in the light from the pathway lamps outside. Her hair slid across her face. I said, "What's your name?"

The girl rustled. She ran her hand over her face. Her hair slid over her face again. She didn't bother with it. She mumbled, "Don't worry about my name."

I got up. My arms and legs looked pale in the naked cold. I crossed the room to the stereo and dropped the needle on an LP in the dark. It turned out to be *Aja* by Steely Dan. Jordan called them platters. He called his weed Mary Jane. He had a name for everything. I dug out his Mary Jane and his pipe, hidden behind the platters. I knew where the fuck my roomie hid the Mary Jane.

The girl had fallen asleep again. She was pretty, with blonde hair and clear pale skin. She had found her sweater and was holding it to her face, cuddling it like a baby blanket. The sweater was soft pink wool. I could tell pink in the dark. My sister had a pink sweater too.

I sat on the bed and lit up a victory bowl. Let the girl sleep without a name, for all I cared. I had done the deed. The one motherfucking deed. The hot smoke warmed me, and I believed I would never want again. I exhaled. Surely goodness and mercy would follow me all of my days. I anointed the girl's cheek with a kiss.

The girl was not asleep. She sat up, and the sweater fell away, and we sat naked in the cold and smoked the weed. We skillfully passed the pipe and the lighter back and forth. I watched the girl. She was pretty, but she was no Theta girl, that's for sure. She was no Caitlin Michaels. But I didn't need a reflection in the window to tell me I was no Jordan.

I said, "Wait a minute. If Jordan's a fairy—"

She glared at me, hard enough to shut me up. I could see her eyes shining in the dark. I didn't understand. If a girl snuck into Jordan's room to cop his Mary Jane and his tequila and spin some platters, was she giving Jordan something in return? Platters and tequila and weed: were they worth Jordan's semen in the back of her mouth?

As the girl put down the pipe, a medical bracelet flashed on her wrist. I had not seen it before. I reached out to flip it over and read it in the snowy light. She pulled her hand back.

"What's it say?"

"None of your business."

"Well, maybe it says your name. Besides, may I remind you, you were passed out, stone cold. I might have needed to know things."

"It says thyroidectomy, if you must know."

"So you're, like, not a girl anymore?"

"Oh my god." She touched her throat, a reflex.

"Let me see." I pulled back her hand.

The winter light showed a white scar, thin as a pencil line. She said, "Happy now?"

"I'm very happy, as a matter of fact. Aren't you happy?"

She gave me the glare again.

Should have found that bracelet sooner. Should have found it while she was passed out. Jordan would have learned her name. That would have come in handy when I was doing the deed. When I cried out. Her name would have been a nice thing to cry out. I had not cried out.

The LP ended. The girl asked for more music, but we listened to silence. We listened to the storm. I thought of this silence as sacred and generous, but she said it was cruel, a silent storm, a smothering snow.

She got out of the bed. She began to dress. She started with her panties and her jeans, digging them from the bottom of the pile.

I dressed too.

I said, "So how do you know Jordan?"

The girl's glare was a blank stare now.

I said, "I doubt he's coming back tonight."

"Perhaps not." She put on her bra.

I said, "I think I know who you are. Your name is Elizabeth. You hang at the Beta House. I've heard about you."

"Is that so?" She put on her turtleneck and her pink wool sweater. She smoothed her hair. She smoothed the collar of the turtleneck. A single fold.

I said, "No, wait. I take it back. You're too preppy. The penny loafers. The sweater. The cuffs folded back. The yoke."

"The what?"

"That girly part on the sweater. The Fair Isle yoke." I pointed to the design around the neck.

She touched her yoke and said, "What guy knows a Fair Isle? Are you a fairy too?"

I said, "My sister has that sweater. I'm just saying you're not a Beta hag. That's all."

She sat beside me and looked around the foot of the bed. She said, "Perhaps I do go to the Beta House. Sometimes."

I said, "Wait. I got it. You're a Kappa, and your name is Caroline."

She asked me how I knew this, and I said that I didn't, not really, and I said something about maybe having seen her walking with Alice after a class, but I didn't know Alice that well either, and she...

The girl put on her socks and penny loafers. I thought about the deep snow waiting for her. She put on her jean jacket. I thought of the cold.

I said, "There was a party last December... and Jordan... maybe it was you... I don't know. There's a lot of blonde girls around here."

The night was mute and still. The storm had moved on, but it had left its silent mark.

She felt the pockets of her jean jacket and said, "I need my gloves."

She sat on the bed and found Jordan's pipe and lighter. She took another hit.

Holding in her breath, she muttered, "I really want my gloves. Aren't you going to look for them?"

"Just give me a clue. Your name."

She exhaled. "It's a boy's name."

"Morgan."

"No."

"Alex."

"That's a girl's name."

"Cameron."

"What the fuck." She stood and looked for the gloves.

I picked up the tequila and the platters. I would clean the blanket after the girl was gone.

She found her lost gloves on the floor.

I said, "Well, I guess this is it." It was a stupid thing to say.

She pulled a thin scarf out of her jean jacket, white to match the gloves. She unrolled it and began wrapping it around her neck. She said, "Jordan would have offered to walk me home."

I said, "I will walk you home."

"Too late." She added, "Jordan would have kissed me and called me 'baby.'"

"Actually, I did kiss you and call you 'baby.'"

"Jordan would have been Jordan."

"I thought you said he—"

By now she wasn't giving me any kind of look at all. She kept busy with the scarf and said, "I don't even know what to say to that."

I wanted my tongue in her mouth again, as if this would accomplish what words were failing at. I took her shoulders, yanked her close, kissed her, made it happen. Her tongue found mine cooperatively enough. When we were done, she said, "That's better." She wiped her mouth on the back of her glove and said, "Perhaps there is a place for you in the world."

And I knew. I remembered a gang of us sitting in a circle in the grass, and the word "perhaps," and I knew who she was. I said, "Now I remember you. The picnic on the quad. September? We ate ice cream. I remember. You were nice."

She didn't show anything, the same as if she hadn't heard me at all. She looked down.

I said, "My name's—"

"Please, don't. I deeply don't care to know your name."

She knotted the scarf beneath her chin. She pulled her hair from under the scarf and flipped it back.

"Come on now. You were nice."

"I'll scream."

"Okay. Jeez."

First time all night, she looked me straight in the eyes. She said, "Listen, do you want every girl on campus to know you jizzed too fast? I don't need your name, little boy."

I looked down. I would not walk her home. I would do nothing.

"Now please get out of my way."

I didn't move.

"I swear to god, I'll fucking scream."

But I didn't move. And she didn't scream. I said, "You know what? When I found you, you were lying on the floor. On Jordan's rug. On his *Don't you dare spill a damn thing on my—don't even walk on my—don't even look at my—too expensive for you, Pell-grant boy* rug. You were so out, you didn't even made it to Jordan's bed, the bed that is always made, because the dude is always out, always getting laid, not too bad for a so-called fairy, and you must have known he was always out, because you came to cop his weed and spin some platters, and I know it's true because I do it all the time, but I don't give blowjobs for it. And when I tripped over you, you curled tighter into yourself, your arms hugged your ribs, your sweater, your warm pink Shetland wool sweater. Fair Isle. I'll say it. And I knew: you held something that was the opposite of me, something I thought I would want forever and would never have. I nudged you with my foot. I said, 'Get up!' I said, 'Party's over, honey. You're welcome. You're welcome for drinking our fucking fine tequila.' Then I said, 'Hey cunt,' but that was all wrong. Jordan would never say that. He would think it, but he wouldn't say it. As he fucked you. Not me, though. I just wanted to touch your shiny hair. So I touched your hair. Then I picked up your cup and finished off your tequila. And the room was so cold, but the tequila was so warm. This went on for a while, me standing over you, staring at my reflection, drinking tequila, and wondering if I was capable of anything. The room was so cold. I knelt and went through your pockets for any clue to your name. In your jacket I found a condom. I found a room key to the girls' dorm. Lipstick. A security whistle. I found your little ruby ring, the kind of ring a dad gives a girl on her sweet sixteen, but curiously you don't wear it on your finger anymore. I found all these things, but I did not find your name. I did not even find your ID, but maybe you don't need it anymore because once upon a time you fucked the dining-hall checker, and now he lets you slide. By the time I was done, I had touched your hips and your hands and your sweater. The cuffs folded back. Just like that. See, I do have a sister. And you were so cold, you were shaking. And when I carried you to the bed, you leaned in, and I knew that you were on some journey that I was not on and would not ever be on. I laid you on the still waters of the bed on which no one has lain. On the virgin night of snow and cold, I placed a blanket over you. Jordan's Hudson Bay blanket. The fucker. The blanket lay over your body and stirred up the air, and you smelled like flowers. I think it was your shampoo. See, if a guy hasn't been around girls, he forgets about flowers. Then I thought, what if you puked? I tilted your head. Jimi Hendrix choked on his puke, see. I pulled back your hair and felt your tequila breath on my palm. I felt your soft hair, your soft skin. And all I needed was a name to make you a person again. You were Heather, the English major, or Amy, the Delta Gamma girl, or Betsy, the library clerk. I said your name, you would hear your name, wake up, thank me for not fucking you, but you would still ask me to walk you home."

Her breath in the cold air was a sparkling pale cloud. She said, "So you think you're honorable because you carried me off the floor. Before you fucked me."

I said, "And, by the way, your name's Leslie."

Her face was hidden. Her hair had fallen forward. She said, "I don't feel well."

I said her name, "Leslie," because that really was her name, and she gazed up, but her eyes were the pale blue that gazes far away, even when the person is staring right at you. Leslie's eyes were pale blue.

I stepped aside. Leslie let herself out.

I stood at the window and watched for her. Jordan wasn't coming back tonight. Caitlin Michaels might regret that, but she wasn't my problem. Never was. Like I had the ability to do right in the world, protect anyone from themselves. From our frosted window, I scraped an opening and watched Leslie trudge across the snow. Her footprints left a crooked trail, one lone person in the cold blue night. As she neared the end of the quad, she pressed a hand against the stone wall. Maybe she was tired. Maybe she was throwing up. She made shuffling steps, her head bent low. She stumbled, regained her footing, and dragged one shoulder along the wall. Harder, slower, she slogged on. The women's dorm was on the other side of campus. It was so cold that the lamplights sparkled like stars, but I didn't worry about that. My eyes were open, watching the stumbling girl, and there was nothing I could do. Tomorrow, if I saw her in the tray line at breakfast, she would stare right through me. Surely goodness and mercy were mine, not hers.

I decided to call my sister. On Jordan's telephone. Who the fuck had a damn private phone in their room? I sat on Jordan's bed and picked up Jordan's phone and dialed the payphone in my sister's hall. My sister, my magic sister, my sister with her lipstick and her nails. My sister, who I could defeat at any boy thing, arm wrestling, bloody knuckles, mumbly-peg, but what good were boy things? Just last Christmas, my sister was packing for the trip back to school, and so was I, but what I didn't realize was that despite going to the same college, we were heading in opposite directions. I went into her bedroom to cop some weed. She was wearing her pink sweater with the white turtleneck underneath, and jeans and penny loafers. All the girls wore them. Her hair was smooth, rolled under at the neck. She was leaning over her suitcase, and she was stashing a plastic disk of pills beneath her clothes. Her hair had swung forward around her face. She looked at me through her hair and said, "Don't tell."

I didn't know what I was seeing. What was I not supposed to tell? I took a guess, though. I sat on her bed and said, "Tell me what it's like."

"Gross!"

"Come on. Tell me."

She said, "Don't worry. Just make sure you use a rubber. And get out of my room now!"

Leslie and I had not used a rubber.

I was calling the phone in my sister's hall.

A tired voice on the pay phone said, "Hello?"

I said, "Can I talk to Marcie?"

The voice said to hold on.

What did I expect to tell my sister? That I had fucked a girl? That I had got me some poontang? Would I say, "Guess what I did tonight, Marcie?" Would I ask if Marcie had ever been a girl passed out on the floor? In her pink sweater? Hell no! Maybe this was why Leslie had said not to walk her home. She was going where I could never go.

Marcie's voice came on. "What the fuck, Ricky?"

I knew then that I would never tell, and Marcie and I would never be the same again.

I said, "Jordan's at the Theta Ball. With Caitlin Michaels."

"I know, Ricky. So what."

"In a strapless gown, and a condom in her purse. And her hair—"

"Omigod, Ricky. Shut up!"

"So there's a girl coming across the campus. I think you should help her in."

"What?"

"She's wearing a jean jacket. Her name is Leslie. She'll be very cold. We—"

"Shut up, Ricky. There is no Leslie over here. She gave you a fake name. Any girl would do the same. Did she give you a fake phone number too? Is that why you're calling me instead? God, you are so dumb."

"When she comes, tell her my name. She's coming over right now. Bid her lie down. The still waters—"

"Listen. There is no Leslie to tell your stupid name to. It's two in the morning, and there is no Leslie tonight. There is no Leslie forever."

Costume Party

It was over, and Denise, kneeling on the bedroom rug, felt clean enough. She rested her hands in her lap, straightened her spine, and closed her eyes. She smelled Kyle and tasted Kyle, and beneath these salty notes she smelled Cynthia's perfume. She was wearing Cynthia's little black dress, kneeling on Cynthia's rug in Cynthia's bedroom with Cynthia's husband. Denise looked down where the cool silk lay across her thighs. She tugged at the hem to cover her knees, and she tried to think clearly and cleanly about what she had done. She clenched her hands into fists. She had not needed them.

Kyle pulled up his pants and fell back on the bed. "Do you think anyone heard?"

Denise let the silk slide through her fingers. She said, "Nobody heard." She knelt forward on the rug and brought herself up. She felt dizzy from the wine, and she gripped the bedpost. She found her heels beside the bed and put them on and tottered over to the dresser. She slugged down the rest of her wine, slugged down Kyle's wine too, and she swished the last of it around her mouth before swallowing. "Nobody ever hears."

Denise fixed her ringlets of hair in Cynthia's mirror and smoothed the black dress around her hips. It was a sheath dress, sleeveless and cool, with an organdy yoke and hem. Her skin tingled from the cool slippery silk. It was sexy, but she didn't like her skin tingling that way. She wanted her pretty white dress with the empire waist and the white bow and the gathered rayon that swung when she turned. But she had spilled red wine in her lap during the book club and had excused herself. Trying on one of Cynthia's dresses in the bedroom, she had been interrupted by Kyle coming in. The pretty white dress was a puddle of rayon at her feet. She had not read the book anyway.

Denise checked her earrings. Always check your earrings after doing the clean thing. One of them was gone. A dangling pearl, tear-dropped, creamy, milky, shiny. She looked around. She had bought the earrings for herself on her birthday—Tony had forgotten—and now one of them was gone. She kept looking.

Kyle was sitting up and watching her. He said, "We have to find it."

"No, YOU have to find it." Denise fought back tears. She thought of having to kneel again at his feet, combing through the rug's pile to find the earring. She thought of being down on that rug again, silk dress and folded legs, salty taste in her mouth. "You find it, Kyle."

"Jesus, if Cynthia finds it first—"

"Really, Kyle? Sounds like you have a problem to solve." Denise swiped her pretty white rayon dress off the floor, wadded it in her fists, and staggered out the door. She let herself cry, and she tasted salt all over again, and the whole night felt messy, not clean. It was only an earring, a small thing, but it was everything.

"White wine gets out red," Kyle yelled after her. Denise heard a thud as Kyle slid off the bed. At least he was looking.

The living room was an ocean of thick white carpet. The deep pile gave Denise trouble on her heels, and she spread her arms for balance. Everything was bright and white. Books and wine glasses lay about. Cynthia was probably giving the women the grand tour. Denise didn't want to see the nursery anyway. She passed the glass table, the tall candles flickering down. The clean thing had taken longer than she had thought. She passed a wastebasket. She stuffed her rayon dress in it. Nothing gets out red.

Everything about the room was white and glass. The grand piano, its lid propped open, was the one black object in the room. Denise went there. She stood by the black thing. In her black dress. Cynthia's dress.

The living room had two great windows that met at a corner. On a clear night you could see the Rockies, capped in shining snow, but now the sky was a solid cloud. The snow blanketed the patio and bent the bare aspen trees. It was coming down hard.

"Well, there you are!" Cynthia had entered the living room. Denise met Cynthia's eyes in the window's reflection. She felt herself tremble, but she was afraid to look away. Her fingers clenched to hide the tremble.

Cynthia smiled and came over to the piano. She wore a black maternity dress with puffy sleeves and a white Peter Pan collar. She poured a fresh glass of red wine for Denise and held it out to her.

"Drink for both of us."

Denise turned to face Cynthia. She loosened her fists and took the glass with two hands.

Cynthia sat at the piano bench and watched her.

Denise looked at Cynthia's belly. Easier than looking at her eyes. Cynthia's maternity dress was black linen, and the crisp pleats flared around her belly. Her belly was not so large. She would shed the weight quickly.

Cynthia saw where Denise was looking. She said, "Do you want to touch it?" She smoothed the dress over her belly.

"No thanks."

"Oh my gosh, Denise, are you crying?"

"It's nothing. I lost an earring. That's all." Denise touched the cold window and looked out. The snow on the patio was smooth and sparkling. Cold air slid down the window. Denise found her reflection: she wanted to see white rayon, an empire waist with a white bow, blonde hair in ringlets. Too girlish? No, she could pull it off. She fixed the ringlets around her face, felt the empty space where the pearl earring was gone.

"It's really starting to come down," Cynthia said. She was still eyeing Denise's reflection.

"How soon till they plow the road?" Denise looked away. Bent aspen trees.

"Soon enough."

Laughter from the other side of the house.

"Because I want to leave."

More laughter.

Cynthia said, "Ellen brought some weed. They're in the nursery, of all places. I'm sure she wouldn't mind if you—"

"Well, I don't do that sort of thing."

Cynthia patted her belly. "Neither do I." She smiled. "Why don't you sit down, Denise. It's going to be a while."

Denise shifted her legs and faced Cynthia. "Actually, I really need—"

"You look lovely, Denise."

"You're just being nice." Denise's ruined white dress had a big white bow.

"And that dress looks—"

"Don't tell me how sexy your little black dress is."

Cynthia gazed at Denise flatly. "Um…"

"And don't tell me that you'll never fit it again, because you will."

"Well…" Cynthia looked down.

Denise said, "I'm sorry. That was mean. No, it wasn't mean, but it was rude."

Cynthia rested her hands over her belly and said, "Yes, it certainly was."

"Maybe I've had too much."

Cynthia's face brightened with a smile. She had a lovely smile. Maybe it was a fake smile. She said, "Denise, you could make it up by playing something for me. I never play anymore."

Denise took another sip.

"Before the wine kicks in?" Cynthia took Denise's glass away. She flipped through the music on the stand. It was Debussy. She pulled out *Le Cathedrale Engloutie*.

Denise said, "I can't play that thing." Her hands clenched. "I mean, I used to play. I don't know. I'm sure you're so much better than I."

"This is a good one. I bet you play it fine." Cynthia took Denise's hand and coaxed her to sit at the piano bench.

Denise slid next to Cynthia on the bench. Cynthia felt warm beside her. The piano was large and black and shiny. She put her hands on the black enamel finish, then set them in her lap. She leaned forward, her arm brushing Cynthia's arm, and she tried to read the score.

She said, "I took lessons from Mr. Bertrand in high school, but I don't remember. He was a creep, I remember that much."

"Oh, I thought he was the best."

Denise said nothing.

Cynthia said, "Look what Debussy wrote here: *dans une brume doucement sonore*. Something about a sweet mist. Can you speak French, Denise? You have a French name."

"No."

"Mr. Bertrand told me what it means. And it's true. It's like that. When he played it for me. Did he ever play it for you, Denise?"

"No."

Cynthia flipped through the scores. She produced *The Girl with the Flaxen Hair*. She tilted her head and looked at Denise. She looked at Denise's face longer than Denise expected. She said, "It's got fewer notes. It might be easier for you right now."

Denise said, "I used to play for my baby. Before the miscarriage, I mean. They say a baby can hear, even inside the womb."

"I'm sorry." Cynthia's face fell. "I'm so sorry. This was a bad idea."

"It's nothing." Denise reached for her wine. "I used to sit forward and press my abdomen against the keyboard so he could hear."

"He?"

"Yeah."

"I'm so sorry."

"But we'll try again. Tony wants to."

"Your Tony is a good guy."

"When he's not away in Chicago." Denise wondered if her cheeks were flushed. Red wine did the trick. She turned and looked at herself in the window. It was stupid to talk about it.

"The thing is," Cynthia took Denise's hands. Her voice was soft. "Everyone has one." She squeezed.

Denise remembered something very old. Mr. Bertrand sitting beside her on the bench and holding her hands. She pulled her hands away.

Cynthia's voice came back. She said, "That doesn't make you feel any better, does it? I mean, I miscarried before this one took, so I know it hurts. That's what I want to say. I had everything picked out. Pink. And now this one's going to be a baby boy." She looked down at her belly. She stroked her linen dress. She said, "To tell the truth, it was kind of a sore spot between Kyle and me."

Denise looked at Cynthia. "You and Kyle don't have any sore spots."

Cynthia's face reflected a sad private thought. Then her face brightened. Her pretty smile came back. "So, Debussy, I could listen to him all night."

"Um, he's great."

"Better than Chopin."

"Better than Ravel."

Denise opened the Debussy score and played *The Girl with Flaxen Hair*. Cynthia leaned warmly against her and followed the score and turned pages for her. There was a difficult part where it built to a crescendo, and there were some wide chords Denise couldn't span. She stumbled through, smoothed it over. She laid her hands in her lap. Fists.

"Sorry."

"It was good, Denise." Cynthia took Denise's hands again and thought for a moment. She said, "Look, I shouldn't have pretended to know, but it must have hurt you badly."

"The DNC is what got me." It was hard to fit the letters in her mouth. D–N–C.

"Yeah."

"And we'll try again."

"I'm just really sorry." Cynthia stroked Denise's hands.

Too loudly, Denise said, "Mr. Bertrand did show me Debussy, but he said my hands were too small to play it."

Cynthia said, "He showed me all this stuff too. He was so good."

Denise said, "His students were all the cute girls."

Cynthia laughed. "Why, thank you. Omigosh, just look at you. Look at me." She giggled. "Look at us cuties." She pointed at their reflection in the second glass wall. They wore black dresses. They held hands.

Denise said, "He used to close his eyes and hum along. Like a moan."

Cynthia said, "That's actually a compliment. He was rapt. Like Glenn Gould. He never did that when I played."

"And he held my hands. I've never told that to anyone. It was creepy. Here I am getting all confessional with you."

"Let's drink a toast," Cynthia said. She lifted Denise's glass. "It's okay for me to have one sip. To Debussy."

"To Debussy," Denise said. She took the glass and had a big slurp. "To the girl with the flaxen hair."

"To all lovely girls," Cynthia said. She took another sip.

"To the first snow of the season." Denise took another sip.

Cynthia said, "To Mr. Bertrand."

Denise took the glass and set it down.

Cynthia leaned her head very close. "Play something else."

Denise played *Le Cathedrale Engloutie.* The piece called for long reaches to the low notes, then very high, reaching across Cynthia's lap to get them, and Denise bumped Cynthia's belly. The music built to a huge crescendo. Denise could do it. She really was good. Had been good. She made a few mistakes, sure, maybe because of the wine, or maybe her hands really were too small, but she was damn good. She felt warm from the wine. And the silk dress made her skin tingle, the silk sheath dress, no empire waist, no bow, not white, not pretty, too sexy, too sleek, Mr. Bertrand's hands in her lap, red wine, not clean, Kyle moaning her name. She stopped abruptly. Fists.

She turned and found Cynthia's eyes. "He really loves you."

"Who?" Cynthia said. "Mr. Bertrand?"

"No, silly. I saw Kyle when I went up to change. I mean, it's okay that we talk. I've known him, like, as long as you have. He really, really loves you." Denise stood. The dress fit perfect on her waist and around her ribs, and it slid coolly against her hips.

Cynthia said, "What are you getting at?"

Denise felt cold in the sexy black dress. She said, "Actually, he's going to surprise you with a trip." The bodice gripped her ribs, and her bare shoulders felt cool. Her skin tingled. The silk dress slid against her skin.

"Where?"

"Where do you want to go?" Denise fought tears.

Cynthia didn't say anything.

"He'll take you there. He likes to dance with you. He likes to cook with you."

Denise's hands were tight fists again. Cold. She wanted Cynthia to take her hands.

"And, oh my gosh, it sounds like you guys have a great sex life. To hear him tell it, anyway. And your bedroom. Wow."

"Denise."

"Did you know I don't even read the books? I read the backs, maybe."

"Denise, please."

"And you'll be a good mom," Denise was whispering now. "And you're sexy. And you don't even need to bleach your hair. You don't even work out. You'll look great in a tight sweater, soon enough again."

Cynthia's eyes narrowed. She was still very pretty. Denise had to turn away, her neck muscles tense. "Did he like you in this dress, Cynthia? Did he kiss you hard? Did he put his hands right here? And down here? Did you like it this way? Did he fuck you, or did you slide down on him and do the clean thing? Did he take your hands, or did he clench your pretty hair in his fists and leave your hands alone?"

Cynthia said nothing.

"Did he cry out your name? Cyn-thi-a…" She liked Cynthia's name in her mouth, on her tongue. "Cyn-thi—" She began to sob. She said, "I'm sorry. This was a mistake. I mean, not a mistake, but—"

"Denise."

Denise gazed out the great glass windows. She saw flashing yellow light and a cloud of snow arching over the embankment as a snowplow with a blower crawled past. She said, "There was this other time, I lost an earring. Mr. Bertrand found it under the piano. And he's like, 'Here. Let me.' And he reaches up to put it back on. His fingers were warm. I flinched, and he's like, 'Little bird, little bird.' I remember his fingers lifting my hair. I remember him leaning against me. His hands were shaking, fumbling. His hands were too big. I held my head still. And then he takes my hands and says, 'Too small. You will never be a great pianist for me. Too small. But always my little bird.'"

The snowplow passed.

Denise turned. She was alone. Cynthia had left the room.

Laughter from the far side of the house.

The snow bent the aspen trees.

Denise would go home now. She would drive alone through the storm, her small hands on the wheel. When she got home, she would listen to Tony on the answering machine. Feel her earring rattle against her skin, the stiff ringlets of hair against her neck. She would go home and sit at her black spinet piano and hack her way through Debussy and wonder why Mr. Bertrand had said those things. He had taken her hands in his and said they were too small. She would play her small piano with her small hands and rest her small fists in her lap and feel clean about it. She was thirty-three and a big girl now, and she had done it plenty of times.

Buena Vista (Part VI)

Sam smelled lemon cleaner and furniture oil. The windows were open, and the fan was humming. Jill lay in bed, reading the book and making notes in the back. Sam sat on the edge of the bed and kissed her cheek. He wondered if Jill knew what that kiss meant, or maybe it was just another thing you did without meaning anything.

He said, "The party was a dud."

"I know about your party."

He wanted to say, *No you don't*, but she probably did. She didn't possibly know everything, but she knew something.

She said, "So are you done? Can we talk about this book now?"

Sam closed Jill's book and took it away. He took her pencil away.

Jill kept her eyes open when they made love. She found Sam's eyes. It was love. But it was love and pain and it ought to be only love. Sam lifted her legs over his waist, just like he'd said. Pressed hard just like he'd said. Sam and Jill held each other's gaze a long time after.

Jill broke it off and sat up. She switched on the light and found the book. She found her notes in the back. Her hair had slipped out of its ponytail. Her hair was smooth and straight and pretend blond, with angled bangs that covered one eye.

Sam said, "The book's no good. It's all made up."

"No, Sam." Jill wrote something in the margin and bit her lip. She said, "By the way, you're changing the sheets tomorrow. First thing. Hospital corners."

Sam looked at the ceiling. "Sparrow Petrosyan was there."

"Did you fuck her?" Jill turned a page.

"What?"

"Did you ever fuck her?"

"Of course I fucked her." Sam was staring at the blank ceiling.

"And?"

"Do you want a comparison? Do you want to be relieved by what you hear? What do you want me to say?"

"I don't really care. You're the one who fucked her. What do you want to say?"

"Do you want to know what it was like?" His eyes found the crack in ceiling plaster.

"Were you happy? Did you two love each other?"

Sam sighed.

Jill said, "Well? You're not even looking at me."

Sam closed his eyes.

"One thing."

"Yes?"

"Open your eyes and listen to me."

"I'm listening."

"I want you to look at me."

"Fine." Sam looked at her.

Jill tucked back her long, slanted bangs. "There's only one reason we're having this conversation. Because nothing else matters anymore, because we totally see through each other's bullshit, each other's scripts and lines and ploys. We have that together. That's something we have."

"Um, yeah."

"And you're not just fucking me anymore. You're not, Sam. Don't fuck me just because we're married. No. Only fuck me when you can't stand holding back anymore. Fuck me when you want to come inside me more than anything in the world. Fuck me when it hurts just to think about it. But don't you dare pretend it's anything more than fucking."

"It's always more." Sam looked around the room, the armoire, the lighting, the mirror, everything.

"Look at me, honey. There's no playing house anymore. There's no bullshit. Someday, I might decide I like you again."

"I like you, enough."

"Shut up."

"Like you enough to do this." He crossed his leg over hers. He slid his hand over her thigh and between her legs. It was warm, but it wasn't enough, and for the first time maybe that was a good thing. He would wait until he wanted it more.

Jill pulled away. "Just listen to the book, Sam. You need to know what happens. I'll read it to you."

Wood

Some vacation. Who expected rain in June? They lay on their bed at the Gold Beach Motel, their bodies twitching from the cool air that split them apart. They gazed at knotted paneling in place of sky.

Darn good thing they'd bought the myrtlewood chess set at the roadside stand. The man set it up on the bedspread and invited the woman to practice endgames.

Calm click of wood on wood.

Patter of rain on the other side of the ceiling.

The woman slid a pawn two spaces and said, "I have no idea what I'm doing."

"We played on our honeymoon, remember?" He took the pawn with his knight.

"No, darling, I don't."

"It was a plastic set. We couldn't afford the good stuff. We played on a bed just like this." He waved his hand. "Maybe this very same room."

The woman rolled onto her back, looked the ceiling over.

The man played with a deliberation that made the woman sigh. It was only a game, damn it, and the honey burls in the grain impelled the woman to touch the pieces and disturb assignations of rook and queen. She put the pieces on squares where they did not belong, and the man grumbled.

She never gave his game a chance. He swept the pieces off the board and set it up fresh.

"Try again?"

Raindrops stuck to the cold window. In the gray light, the pieces cast faint shadows across the board. When the man and woman were twenty, they had chased each other's long shadows on the golden sand.

She turned the yellow king between her thumb and forefinger.

"Pretty."

"Yeah, they carve them on a lathe."

"I know."

"They call it myrtlewood, but where we live, it's a—"

"California bay, darling. Now what else do you have for me?"

"Don't ask unless you really want to know." He took the king from her, tumbled the pieces into the box, and pit-ter-pattered his fingers on the box like rain. She rubbed her fingers together, where the tallest chess piece used to be.

Myrtlewood's soft warm notes did not last long.

Somalia

The sun settled over the water, and the first twinkling stars, two or three of them, took their places in the darkening sky. Perfect night for a bonfire on the beach. Pound a few beers with the guys. Talk about old times. David tried to settle into his camp chair. He tried to find a place for his gaze to rest. He found his wife, Alyson, her silhouette, and he found the other wives' silhouettes, gathering at the water's edge, and he found the children, their restless silhouettes shifting in and out of the tide. The sun shimmered on the water, but not for long. "One more hour," David said. It was a statement of time, and it would come true whether he said it or not. He settled his gaze on the restless, flickering fire.

David's old pal Adams stood up and poked the fire with a stick. "So, my good gentlemen, which one of us will get laid tonight?"

David listened to the lapping waves. He watched the sparks rise into the sky.

Adams said, "Come on. Speak. Who's getting some?" He poked the fire again.

David looked across the sand to Alyson. Her silhouette was tucking back her hair. Her hair blew loose again. David watched for her to tuck it back again.

Bobby said, "Are you asking because you want to brag? Or are you taking bets?"

Charlie downed his beer and said, "Maybe he wants to spy through a knothole."

Good old Charlie!

Adams poked his stick into the fire and said, "Tell you what. If I do get laid tonight, gentlemen, can it be with someone else's wife?"

"Dude," said Bobby. He stared up at Adams from his camp chair and grinned.

David sipped his beer and listened to the waves and watched the fire.

Adams said, "By the way, I think we all know which wife I'm talking about."

Charlie said, "Watch yourself, pal." He stood from his chair. He glared at Adams across the fire.

Adams said, "Relax, dude, we are so not going there." He tossed his stick into the fire.

"Better not," said Charlie.

"The man told you to relax, okay?" Bobby stood and glared at Charlie. He inhaled at the end of his words. He wasn't relaxed. He glanced sideways at Adams, maybe for approval, but Adams wasn't watching.

Charlie sat down.

Bobby sat down.

Adams found another stick to poke at the fire. "So, my good gentlemen..."

David stretched his legs toward the heat. He didn't say anything. He didn't say, "I'm getting laid tonight. Alyson and I are going to fuck. I'm going to come inside her, and she's going to want it and beg for it, pleading in my ear, and I will be coming hard because I want it too. Of course, this does not mean we are happy. But why do we need to be happy, anyway?" David didn't say that. He said, "Just to be clear, we're not good gentlemen."

Adams and Bobby held their beers high and cried, "Hear, hear!"

Charlie opened another one, too late for the toast. He wagged his bottle in the empty air.

Poor Charlie.

The golden water flashed. The children jumped the waves. Whenever a big wave roared in, the children ran from it. David's son, Dylan, was out there, and David spotted him, the silhouette with raggedy hair. The women were supervising the children. Their arms were folded. They wore thin summer sweaters and Capri jeans. David watched as they turned from the children to greet a woman walking up the beach. The woman wore a wide skirt that caught the breeze and rippled in the fading sunlight.

Bobby said, "Hey, Charlie, isn't that Carolyn? Your Carolyn?"

Adams said, "Is she hot? If she's hot, then it's Carolyn."

Charlie said, "You think I'm not serious, asshole? Watch yourself."

Bobby said, "The thing I don't get is why she always goes off by herself."

David said, "A woman can take a walk if she wants to."

The women by the waves gathered around Carolyn. Carolyn's hands moved as though she were telling a story. Even in silhouette you could tell it was a good story, and the other women leaned close. One woman lifted her hand to her chin. Another woman touched Carolyn's arm. But David could tell that his wife, Alyson, was not riveted by the story. Alyson was looking down, extending her toes and dragging them in the sand. She looked up at Carolyn, then back down. The sunlight flickered through her loose hair. She turned back to the children.

Bobby said, "Hey Charlie, they're talking about you."

"What?"

"You know, they tell each other everything."

David said, "Not everything." He sipped his beer. He didn't watch anymore.

Bobby said, "The ironic thing is, there's nothing to tell, is there, Charlie?"

Charlie said, "You looking to get thumped, asshole? There'll be something to talk about after I—"

Adams said, "Shut up, both of you."

David watched Alyson's silhouette as it moved away from the other women. Alyson waded tiptoe in the shallow water, up to her calves, and she waved Dylan in from the tide, and he came running. Holding hands, Alyson and Dylan trudged in. As they neared the men, Alyson cast David a long look. Her loose hair was tangled from the breeze. It was a long sad look.

Bobby said, "Fuck was that supposed to mean?"

David said nothing. Turning his head, he watched Alyson and Dylan pass the men and climb the steep stairs to the cabin.

Adams said, "I suppose we should go out there and supervise. The kids and the waves and all."

"Yeah," Bobby said.

"We'll get in trouble if we don't," Adams said. "Maybe there's even a sleeper log in the waves."

"Yeah," Bobby said, "a sleeper."

Charlie said, "But the women are watching the kids."

"No, they're not. Not really."

"Then fuck it." Charlie added a log to the fire. "I say fuck it."

David watched the log surrender to the heat. He pulled back his legs, the heat too much for his shins.

After the crashing of what seemed like a hundred ocean waves, Adams spoke. "Charlie, that's the smartest thing you've ever said."

"What did I say?"

A new silence lasted another hundred waves.

Adams said, "Did anyone bring stuff for s'mores? Bobby? Any graham crackers and Jet-puff marshmallows in that magic bag of yours? You know, for the children? S'mores for the children buys a lot of cred with the wives."

Bobby dug his hand into the bag and grinned. "Just the fireworks. The grownup kind from the rez."

Adams said, "We are so bad."

Bobby held out his beer for a clang and a "Hear, hear," but he didn't get one.

Charlie said, "It's pronounced *ma-low*."

Adams said, "Fuck you say?"

Charlie scowled at the fire. His arms were folded. "It's *marsh-ma-low*, spelled with an *a*, so it's marsh-*ma*-low."

"Yeah, well *asshole* is spelled with an *a* too, so why don't you stick a 'marsh-*ma*-low' up yours."

"I'm just saying."

"You're just saying bullshit."

"I'm trying to have a little fun, man. Levity, you know."

"No fun for you, dude. No fun for you and your beautiful wife."

Charlie stood, stepped right over Bobby in his chair, and squared off against Adams.

"Take that back."

"The beautiful part?" Adams didn't blink.

"Fuck you." Charlie kicked at the sand. He went back to his chair and sat down. Charlie was much skinnier than Adams. He opened another beer and gripped it to his chest.

Adams said, "So, David, good seeing you. What's it been, ten years? A lot of catching up. Let's start with this. Are—you—getting—laid—tonight?" He handed David a fresh bottle and met his eyes.

David thought Adam's eyes looked tired. He took the beer. Beyond Adam's shoulder, he saw Carolyn coming toward them from the water, her skirt flickering in the breeze. He pointed and said, "Saved by the bell."

Adams turned and watched Carolyn and said, "You mean saved by the *belle*. Seriously, Charlie, all ribbing aside, your wife is so hot."

"Fuck you," Charlie said. His hands gripped his beer, and he stared at the fire, his eyes becoming a glaze.

Everyone turned toward Carolyn as she drew closer, and Bobby said softly, "Okay, Charlie, now you are in trouble."

Carolyn came up. The dry, loose sand made her walk slowly as she selected her steps, her graceful arms floating out for balance, her hips swinging. She wore the wide skirt and a thin cardigan sweater, buttoned up. Her smooth blonde hair made an even line at her neck, and her hair shone in the firelight. She looked down, and her hair slid forward, and she did not tuck it back.

She said, "Hello, good gentlemen."

The men chuckled.

She said, "Oh my. I didn't know I was so amusing." Her hand rose to her hair. She turned and said, "Hello, Charlie, honey."

Charlie said, "Did you have a nice walk? I'm pretty sure none of our kids drowned while you were gone."

"My walk was delightful." Carolyn inched closer to the fire, but instead of going to Charlie, she sat on the armrest of David's folding chair. David felt the chair tip a little. Carolyn's arm slid around him.

Bobby said, "Uh oh."

Carolyn took David's beer and sipped it. She leaned close. She smelled like flowers. Her hand pressed on his back. David felt a rush of memory as when you bite into a rare peach after not having eaten one in a long time.

Bobby grinned and said it again, "Uh oh."

Carolyn said, "What? Is there a problem? I'll have you know that David and I are old friends. This doesn't mean anything." She squeezed David closer. "David loves Alyson, and Charlie loves me. Don't you, Charlie."

"Sure, baby." He glared at the fire.

Adams said, "And Carolyn, who do you love?"

David drank his beer. He thought about Carolyn's skin. He thought of flowers.

Carolyn said, "You know, there was a time, back in college, when David and I thought we were going to be married. But we were very young, and we could say those things, couldn't we, baby, and it didn't matter because we knew it would never come true. And he's still my baby, right, and I can say that because it doesn't matter."

Charlie said, "Carolyn, stop it."

"That sounds like a corrective, honey. Do you see anything here that needs correcting?" Her hand made a graceful flourish down her body. "Everything here is perfect and correct. What needs correcting is you and me, Charlie."

Charlie said, "Carolyn, you need to go."

"Don't tell me what to do. I'm talking with my old friend. With David, my dear old friend. You do remember, don't you? David and I used to—"

"Carolyn—" Charlie's voice rose.

"Right here on this beach. In fact, this one time—"

"Hush."

"No, you hush!" She stood. "I'm going now because I want to, not because you told me to. Everything I do is something I want to do. Goodbye, everyone. Goodbye, David." She bent and kissed him. Her wet mouth sealed with his. She walked away.

"Well, I think we all know who is NOT getting laid tonight."

"And I think we know who is."

"Perfect and correct, indeed."

David was lost to the talk about who was getting laid. He was lost to the ribbing. He ground his heels into the sand. Carolyn triggered a regret so profound he could not speak of it, and he tried to hide the regret by keeping his face very still, his eyes gazing at the fire. Then he checked the men's faces. They were gazing at the fire too.

They listened to the restless waves.

Adams said, "You know, on the other side of the earth, sitting around a campfire under the stars, there is a guy on a beach in Somalia who will never have this. He will never have what we have."

Charlie said, "Actually, it's mid-morning in Somalia."

"What do we have, Adams?" David said. "What the fuck do we have?"

Bobby said, "We have beautiful women. Don't we have beautiful women?"

"Not just that," Adams said. "We have it all. Compared to that Somali guy, we have the richness of kings. But somehow, tonight, I don't feel rich."

Bobby said, "Charlie, you feeling rich?"

Charlie said nothing. He gave Bobby the finger.

Adams poked at the fire. He continued. "Think about it. You could be fired tomorrow. Your wife could leave you. A sleeper log could wash over the kids. But don't talk about it. I shouldn't talk about it even now. Just keep on doing. Savor every moment. Drink your beer. This, the Somali could appreciate."

Charlie said, "They're Muslims, and they don't drink."

David said, "Tell me, does this man in Somalia regret what he has?"

"He doesn't have anything. He's in fucking Somalia."

Bobby cried, "Somalia!" He held out his beer.

Carolyn came back. The sun was down now. Her slow, beautiful walk made a silhouette, and then the breeze caught her skirt, and the sun filled it with light.

She came into the light of the fire and said, "Somalia?"

"To Somalia."

She sat on the armrest of David's chair. "I want to hear about Somalia." She took David's hand. Her skin was soft.

The memory of her softness burst on David again.

Bobby said, "I want to hear more about David and Carolyn."

Charlie said, "Well, our resident asshole Adams was just saying not to feel sorry for yourself. For what you have. For all the good things you goddamned have."

Carolyn's hand gripped tighter. Warm and soft and familiar.

Bobby said, "What Adams is saying is that it's time for Charlie and David to duke it out over Carolyn."

Adams said, "Is that what I'm saying? Look at you."

Charlie said, "No, you're saying that it's pointless to want anything. To want more than we have. Because you could lose it in a snap."

David said, "I concur with Adams."

Carolyn said, "What if you don't like what you have?"

Adams said, "Carolyn, you're a good Republican. You protect your kin. You guard your stake. Everything that is fine and good could be taken from you tomorrow. You are just like our man in Somalia. Well, not you, exactly. I mean certainly not you. Not you in particular. I mean—vavoom— not you. Jesus Christ. What the hell do I mean?"

David said, "Be polite, Adams."

"What, so I got to wait for her to leave before I can speak my mind?" Adams opened another beer.

Charlie said, "I want to hear more about the 'everything fine and good' part, because apparently I am missing out on all of that."

Silence. A single wave crashed.

Carolyn nuzzled David and spoke softly in his ear. "Fine and good, baby. That could have been us. Do you ever think about that? Do you?"

David looked at Carolyn. He let his face show his sadness. He softly said, "Do I ever think about us? That's very fine and good to think about. When I'm sad about what I do have, that's exactly what I think about." He looked toward

Charlie, then back at Carolyn. "You're so right: it could have been us. Miserable me and miserable you."

Silence.

David wished he could take it back.

Carolyn stood. She gathered her wide skirt and walked around the fire. She took poor Charlie's hand and helped him up. He stumbled. She yanked his arm, and they trudged toward the water. Then she looked back, her foot twisting in the sand. She let go of Charlie, she let him stumble and fall, and she stomped back to the fire. She yelled, "You know what, David? Know what? You waited for me to want the things you wanted, but then you stopped waiting, so don't cut me down for saying I want them now." She turned and walked away for good, Charlie stumbling beside her.

Adams said, "Nice work. Lovely thing. You scared her away."

Carolyn and Charlie were silhouettes at the edge of the tide, trudging past the other wives, splashing into the water. Charlie's silhouette spread its legs and peed. Carolyn gathered her skirt, waded out to the children, and motioned them in, her arm sweeping, yanking against the dark air.

Bobby said, "I'm glad you scared her away. I can watch her legs and her waist and her hips. Oh man. Scare her away again and again."

Adams said, "Seriously, what's the story, David?"

Bobby said, "Yeah, what's the story? Spill it."

David didn't know what the story was. These guys only wanted to hear what might have been, and he didn't know anything about that. He said the first thing that came into his restless mind. He said, "When my wife, Alyson, was a little girl, she was jumping the waves, a night just like this, probably. I don't know. Anyway, a big wave went out and sucked her under. She basically drowned, and she saw the white light at the end of the corridor, you know what I'm saying? Next thing she remembers, her dad and a stranger, a woman, are holding her upside down to shake out the sea-water. Then they set her down in the sand, and she's crying, and this strange woman, not her mom, is comforting her. Check this out: Alyson nearly drowned, and she doesn't know where her mom is, and this other woman held her and cooed to her and stroked her face, and Alyson had to take it. Where was her mom? Was her dad having an affair with the woman? Alyson doesn't know. Her mom and dad divorced a few months later."

David stood. He tossed his bottle into the fire. He said, "The most interesting story is the choices you make, not the choices you don't. And, with that being said, I'm off to fuck my wife. I'm off to protect my kin, like Adams says. Do Alyson and I fight? Hell yes. Are there regrets? Yes. And maybe that's what makes it the most interesting choice. So tell Charlie, yeah, I fucked his wife, but that was a long time ago, and now I'm going to fuck mine."

Bobby's eyes shone like a puppy's. "Dude..."

David turned back to the fire. "And when we're done, Alyson will talk. You know she'll want to talk. God damn, she likes to talk. She'll snuggle up real close against my side, and I'll be so tired, and she'll start in. She'll say, 'Everyone says Carolyn's so pretty. So hot. Is she really hot?' And I'll hold her close and say, 'No.'"

Adams sighed and raised his eyes to speak, but David quickly said, "Shut the fuck up, both of you." He met their eyes in turn. "And then she'll say it again, 'Is Carolyn hot?' but I won't budge. Finally, she'll move on. She'll say, 'Bobby's a fairy, you know,' but I won't know. And then she'll say, 'Adams loves his wife so much. He'd have to love her just to put up with her.' See, they do tell each other everything, right? Except the bit about me and Carolyn: you see, Alyson doesn't actually know about me and Carolyn. I mean she does know. She's not dumb. Of course she knows. But we tell each other a story with no Carolyn in it, a true sad story that happened this way, not that way, and we tell it over and over. So excuse me, good gentlemen. I'm going off to tell that story now."

Carolyn and Charlie were trudging up from the waves, their children in tow. Adams' wife and Bobby's wife came in with their children too. It was pitch dark now, and it was cold, even near the fire, and the grownups held the children close. Bobby tore open his reservation fireworks and poked their shafts upright in the sand. Adams poked the fire.

David left the fire and walked up the beach toward the cabin. As he neared the wooden stairs, he thought he saw Alyson standing on the balcony, a silhouette against the cabin's big, bright windows. David heard Adams yell for everyone to stand back, stand the hell back, damn it, and David turned. Bobby lit the first fuse with a stick from the fire. It was a dud. Those reservation fireworks often were. He lit the second one. The rocket shot up, exploding in the air, bright as day, lighting faces where sadness and regret and joy and wonder equally played.

Acknowledgments

One of the reviewers praised this collection for being lean and precise. Therefore, I will be brief in these acknowledgments. Let me begin with thanking the editors of the literary magazines who first published stories from this collection. Next, thank you to my writing group (Amber, Chad, Amy, Steph, and Quinn) for giving "Noise" a thorough critique. And thank you to Linera Lucas for pointing "Costume Party" in the right direction. Thank you to Ken Post for our many discussions about realism in general and writing about the West in particular. Finally, I must depart from leanness and precision to effusively thank the awesome staff of Cornerstone Press: Dr. Ross K. Tangedal, Director & Publisher, for making me feel heard at every stage but also for keeping me on task; Scott Miller for the bang-up cover design; Karlie Harpold and her team of eagle-eyed editors for asking all the right questions; and Sam Bjork and Sophie McPherson in media and sales. I cannot imagine a smoother path to publication.

* * *

The author wishes to acknowledge the following publications, where stories appeared in earlier versions:

"Egg and Dart", "The Stick Up": *Timberline Review*
"Down the Mountain": *ZYZZYVA*
"Repair Job": *Weber: The Contemporary West*

"The Hiding Place": *Clackamas Literary Review*
"Soft and Warm Against Me": *Variant Lit*
"Don't Tell Me About Bosnia": *Digital Americana;* reprinted in *Sequestrum*
"Snowy Day": *Pinyon*
"Anasazi": *Manifest West*
"Don't Say Anything": *Lunch Ticket*
"Costume Party": *New Madrid*
"Wood": *North Coast Squid*
"Somalia": *Main Street Rag*
"Buena Vista": *Roi Faineant*

EVAN MORGAN WILLIAMS is an award-winning story writer. A 2024 Oregon Literary Fellow in Fiction and a recipient of the Laurell Swails and Donald Monroe Memorial Fellowship, he has published over seventy-five short stories in literary magazines, including *The Kenyon Review, ZYZZYVA, Alaska Quarterly Review, Witness,* and *The Antioch Review.* He has published three collections of short stories: *Thorn* (2014), winner of the gold medal from the Independent Publishers Book Awards; *Canyons | Older Stories* (2018), winner of the gold medal from the Next Generation Independent Book Awards; and *Stories of the New West* (2021). Williams holds an MFA from the University of Montana, and he is a three-time mentor in AWP's Writer to Writer Mentorship Program. He is retired after twenty-nine years of public school teaching.

www.ingramcontent.com/pod-product-compliance
Lightning Source LLC
Chambersburg PA
CBHW020035310726
48970CB00007B/2268